Appalachia (un)Masked

Volume 25 - 2022

Pine Mountain Sand & Gravel
Contemporary Appalachian Writing

Contemporary Appalachian Writing

Volume 25: 2022

Appalachia (Un)Masked

Coeditors: Sherry Cook Stanforth (Managing Editor),
   Jim Minick & Dana Wildsmith

Book Reviews Editor: Edwina Pendarvis

Layout & Design: Elizabeth H. Murphy - Illusion Studios
   Typeset in Adobe Garamond Pro & Gilligan's Island

Editorial Intern: Rielle Long

Administrative/Editorial Assistant: Pamela Hirschler

Founding Editor: Jim Webb

Founding Publisher: Robb Webb

PMS&G logo courtesy of Colleen Anderson of *Mother Wit*
Front Cover: *Gatlinburg, Tennessee #2* by Chuck Billingsley
   (Digital photograph)

Pine Mountain Sand & Gravel. Copyright 2022 to the authors herein and to *PMS&G*. *Pine Mountain Sand & Gravel* is a publication of the Southern Appalachian Writers Cooperative (SAWC), whose mission is to encourage, support, and publicize the work of members and friends. With the exception of literary or scholarly review, no material may be reproduced in whole or in part without permission from *PMS&G* and the author (who retains all publication rights). For ordering and information contact: pmsg.journal@gmail.com.

Published in cooperation with Dos Madres Press

www.dosmadres.com

Dos Madres Press, Inc. is an Ohio Not For Profit Corporation and a 501(c)(3) qualified public charity.
Contributions are tax deductible.

This project was supported in part by Johnson Controls Foundation Matching Gift Program and anonymous donors.

ISBN 978-1-953252-67-8
Library of Congress Control Number: 2022945733

For ordering and information contact:
pmsg.journal@gmail.com

PINE MOUNTAIN SAND & GRAVEL CO.
Whitesburg, Kentucky

NAME _____

For Period Ending _____, 195___

Earnings	No. Of	Rate	Amount
Tons @			
Hours @			
Hours @			
		Total Earnings	

DEDUCTIONS	AMOUNT	
Cash		
W'holding Tax		
S. S. Tax		
Fuel		
U. M. W. of A.		
Supplies		
Transfers		

Total Deductions			
AMOUNT DUE			
Overdraft			
TOTAL DUE EMPLOYEE			
Amount Due Company			

Received of Pine Mountain Sand & Gravel Co., amount shown above in full payment for wages.

Signed: _____

This Check Includes Your
Vacation Pay Bonus.

"Don't worry about the mule going blind, just load the wagon"

Table of Contents

About the Southern Appalachian Writers Cooperative xi
Introduction xiii
Sue Weaver Dunlap — Light Seeker 1
Connie Jordan Green — Morning 2
Gershon Ben-Avraham — Still, They Sing 3
Carol Grametbauer — You Two 4
Wendy McVicker — Anger, waiting 5
Karen Whittington Nelson — Center 6
Mischelle Anthony — Cling 7
Ellen Austin-Li — The Curtain 8
KB Ballentine — When We Get There, I Will Have
    Nothing Left to Tell 10
Victoria Woolf Bailey — The Secret Life of Parents 11
Jim Minick — *Spring Dance* 12
Elissa Yancey — Modern Mother Love 13
Sam Barbee — The Wake 22
Rhonda Pettit — Glass Negative 24
Roy Bentley — "Hey, That's No Way to Say Goodbye" ... 25
Marc Harshman — The Secrets of Family Life 26
Dan Leach — Lockjaw 27
Pam Campbell — Until Death Do Us 37
Kenneth Chamlee — Dark Edge 39
Hilda Downer — The Arrow 40
Natalie Kimbell — On the Pound Near Phillips Creek
    in Virginia 41
Pamela Hirschler — After the Flood 43
Michael Dowdy — When I Shop, I Dream of Rivers of
    Workers Building a Dam 44

vii

Phyllis Price — Winter Roses 46
Nettie Farris — Jane 47
Kari Gunter-Seymour — Legitimate Cockamamie 48
Jessica Weyer Bentley — Leonard's Juliet......................50
Judy Jenks — *The Diner*..51
Preston Martin — Hayride Weather................................52
Ann Thornfield-Long — Whistling the Way Home 53
Sherry Poff — In Secret Places 59
Patsy Kisner — Black Walnut..60
Patricia Hope — The Secret Is… 61
John C. Mannone — The Making of Steel.....................62
Richard Hague — What I Had Instead of Stories..........63
Carson Colenbaugh — Copperhill.................................64
William Scott Hanna — Homecoming.........................66
Mike Templeton — Strata and Flows 67
Tommye Scanlin — *Five Leaves for Miss Lillian* 72
Carol Parris Krauss — The Old Folks Warn You
     About the Willow Tree 73
Taylor Roberts — For the Record 74
Dale Farmer — Never Out of My Heart 75
McKenna Revel — My Mother's Father's First Story.......80
Todd Davis — Where Fisher Go to Die 81
Gabriel Dunsmith — The Raveling................................82
Jackie Ison Kalbli — If My Best Face Forward
     Came Off, ...83
Jim Minick — The Collar..85
Pauletta Hansel — Presidents Day 2021 86
Scott T. Hutchison — Equality.......................................89
Gerald Smith — Omen 91
Elaine Fowler Palencia — Fleeing Eden 93
Chrissie Anderson Peters — Marking...........................95

Mike Schoeffel — My Buddy Evan 96
Sherry Cook Stanforth — 23 and Appalachian Me 99
Michael Thompson — *Ascent* 102
Jerry Buchanan — Song of the Stones 103
John Thomas York — Soul Bus 105
Alexandra McIntosh — Walking the Railroad
    Tracks with Brian Wilson 115
Thomas Alan Holmes — Bristol, TN/VA 116
Damian Dressick — The Road Still Traveled 117
LuLu Johnson — Paso Fino 119
Llewellyn McKernan — Appalachian Love Song 123
Laurie Wilcox-Meyer — Dearest Mother 124
A. Riel Regan — Belief in the City 125
Judy Jenks — Trailer Park Chicks 126
Eugene Stevenson — Heart's Code 130
Ann Shurgin — Percussion, Mid-Pandemic 131
Anna Egan Smucker — Not What He Expected 133
Thomas E. Strunk — A History of the Masks I Wore 134
Kari Gunter-Seymour — *"Uh-Huh, It's Your Birthday"* 142
Allison Thorpe — The Mouth Returns to Civilization 143
Dick Westheimer — There Are No Maskless Men
    Standing in Line at the Local Pharmacy 144
Chuck Stringer — This Year 146
Karla Linn Merrifield — And So On 147
Dottie Weil — The Collar 148
Karl Plank — Grave Stones 152
Denise Roberts McKinney — The White Pine
    Cathedral 155
Roberta Schultz — Bones in the Woods 157
Timothy Dodd — Shenandoah 158
Beth Copeland — Trick or Treat, 1957 159

Chuck Billingsley — *Gatlinburg, Tennessee #1* 160
Ron Houchin — Underworld 161
Ron Houchin — The Longevity of Smoke Rings 162
Pauletta Hansel, Marc Harshman & Jim Minick —
    Remembering Ron Houchin, 1947-2022 163
Dana Wildsmith — Pandora 169
Jennifer Davis Michael — Snakeskin 170
Jay Pettit — [I approached the river] 171
Sherrie Skipper — Pretend I Have No Religion
    and Let Me Write This Poem 172
Bonnie Proudfoot — Look Away 173
Gary Phillips — Weather-Bound 174
Dale Marie Prenatt — General Delivery 176
Matt Prater — For Voyager, Leaving the Solar System 177
Byron Hoot — Meandering in Sanctuary 178

BOOK REVIEWS & NEWS

Thomas Crowe – *Joy Amongst the Catastrophe: The Pandemic,
    Politics, and Climate Change* by Steve Abhaya Brooks 181
Timothy Dodd – *The Land of the Dead is Open for Business*
    by Jacob Strautmann 184
Donna Meredith – *Secure the Shadow* by Michael Henson 187
Philip St. Clair – *The Girl Singer* by Marianne Worthington 190
A. E. Stringer – *When Light Waits for Us* by Hilda Downer 194

NEW BOOKS compiled by Edwina Pendarvis 199

CONTRIBUTORS 207

SUBMISSION GUIDELINES 230

About the Southern Appalachian Writers Cooperative

In 1974, a group of writers and activists gathered at Highlander Center in New Market, Tennessee, to form what became the Southern Appalachian Writers Cooperative. From its very beginning, SAWC was intended to support writers in our efforts to take control of our regional identity and to take action, individually and collectively, on the issues that impact our land and our people.

For over four decades, the Southern Appalachian Writers Cooperative has provided a place for us to come together to share our work and our struggles, and to ponder how these things affect, not only our work, but also our relationships with each other, with the region and with the broader culture. During the 1970s, SAWC sponsored readings and published *New Ground,* an anthology of contemporary Appalachian literature. In the 1980s, the Appalachian Poetry Project, initiated by Gurney Norman with poets George Ella Lyon and Bob Henry Baber, brought new life into SAWC. Poets and writers from throughout the Appalachian region gathered in their own and one another's communities and celebrated together at Highlander Center. SAWC has met (almost) annually since this time, usually at Highlander Research and Education Center and always in the fall. Through this and other SAWC Writers Gatherings and by sponsoring local readings and the literary magazine *Pine Mountain Sand & Gravel,* the Southern Appalachian Writers Cooperative continues its original mission to foster community, activism and publication among Appalachia's writers.

Pine Mountain Sand & Gravel was founded in the

mid-1980s by brothers Jim and Robb Webb. Their company, Appalapple Productions (Jim being a resident of Letcher County, Kentucky, and Robb of the Big Apple) produced three volumes of the journal before passing the torch to the Southern Appalachian Writers Cooperative in 1996. In its thirty-some years of publication, *PMS&G* has produced 25 volumes of contemporary Appalachian writing, and has been stewarded by 14 editors and co-editors. (Starting with Volume 19, young editorial interns also joined the team, reflecting the SAWC value for literary mentorship.) In 2015, the Southern Appalachian Writers Cooperative (in collaboration with Dos Madres Press) also published *Quarried: Three Decades of Pine Mountain Sand & Gravel*. Edited by editor emeritus Richard Hague, *Quarried* showcases early writing by notable Appalachian authors including Lee Howard, George Ella Lyon, Jeff Daniel Marion, Jim Wayne Miller and Gurney Norman, alongside newer work by many of Appalachia's currently established and emerging poets, essayists, and novelists.

Pine Mountain Sand & Gravel is now an annual, themed journal. The current call for submissions, purchase information, a list of upcoming readings, and information about the Southern Appalachian Writers Cooperative's fall and other gatherings can always be found at *sawconline.net*. You may also contact *Pine Mountain Sand & Gravel* at pmsg.journal@gmail.com.

Introduction

Creative pondering around this *PMS&G* Appalachia (Un)Masked theme inspired unique translations of what lies beyond our immediate perception. Stories of curiosity, wonder, confusion, beauty, and terror emerged through the writing and art.

In July, while this book was coming together, Appalachia experienced a devastating event. Deadly flooding evolved due to an unusual, lingering stationary front that brewed up "training thunderstorms" and pounding rain. Wild water soon enshrouded the valley terrain of Eastern Kentucky and beyond, destroying cherished people and homeplaces. No one saw it coming. Once the rivers and streams ebbed, scenes of grief arose from the unmasked ruins.

There is no writing or art capable of translating the distinctive losses in the lives of our regional kin. Beyond the ache of drownings—a contorted, dirty geography...homes drudged in filth, if not twisted by nature's forces...families robbed of drinking water, food, shelter, possessions, and each other. Decades of historical Appalshop archives were ruined by the muddy waters covering Whitesburg, Kentucky. Hindman Settlement School, which has inspired well over a century of educational and cultural arts action, also sustained major damages, even while providing shelter for homeless residents in the area. Troublesome Creek receded to unmask a firetruck jammed beneath its mud-spattered bridge. In fact, in a single night, Central Appalachia became a land of lost bridges.

Trouble steps out of the shadows when we least expect it. But then again, so does hope, embodied in human kindness, support, and determination. As I draft this reflection, people all over the region are organizing, including many of our *PMS&G*

friends, to turn tragedy's paralysis into tangible, practical action. Public language often separates Appalachian people and places from the rest of America, much like a caul, where diverse individuals are *hidden, tucked away, cloaked, buried, walled in, remote, enshrouded, removed, contained*—virtually *lost* beneath a metaphorical veil, or perhaps, literal rubble.

But any notion of *gone*, in the spirit of Si Kahn's iconic song, will be an unmasked, actively engaged Appalachia that is "Gone, Gonna Rise Again." We continue to sing that testimony of resilience:

> High on the ridge above the farm
> I think of my people that have gone on
> Like a tree that grows in the mountain ground
> The storms of life have cut them down
> But the new wood springs from roots in the ground…

Sherry Cook Stanforth
Summer, 2022

This issue of *Pine Mountain Sand & Gravel* is dedicated to
Ron Houchin,
our beloved and longtime friend. 1947-2022.

Appalachia (Un)Masked

Sue Weaver Dunlap
Light Seeker

I count stars, wait dawn, breathe first light crawling
over the ridge. I rest in the solitude of morning,
quiet outside our windows, songbirds not yet ready
to sing sunrise. My ritual of aloneness, counting
blessings, writing letters to God, praise for the cardinals'
redness, color woven into this year of newness, rocks
and roots blocking paths of familiarity. The sameness
of days hold hope, tenacity for this seeker of dawn.

Connie Jordan Green

Morning

> *I am silver and exact.*
> —Sylvia Plath

Flat as the mirror
that hangs on my wall,
this morning lake,
heron on the dock
made double,
my canoe paddle
the only disturbance.

The far bank
spreads a leafy green,
the sun's path a road
my canoe and I travel,
this mirror neither silver
nor exact, but a shifting
surface where all
that's reflected
comes back softer,
more gentle
than the real world
could ever be.

Gershon Ben-Avraham

Still, They Sing

> *I know all the birds of the mountains.*
> —Ps. 50:11

The last thing he wished before the Angel
of Forgetfulness touched his lips was to
be reborn as a bird in these mountains.

He yearned to soar above hills and valleys,
to be born in a nest resting on the
topmost limb of the tallest tree on the
highest hill; to drift into sleep each night,
clinging to a branch rocked by the rhythm of
wind blown in from some hidden darkling sea.

In life, he had trod the earth's flatland paths
with leaden feet and sat upon the banks
of rivers listening to melodies
he hummed and seemed to know from memory.

We buried him back home, in Kentucky,
next to his granny, near the farm he loved,
while birds sang his eulogy. Still, they sing.

In memory of Lynn Turner (1946-2014)
Buried in Pelfrey-Lovelace Cemetery, White Oak, Kentucky.

CAROL GRAMETBAUER
You Two

Buried deep in this early-1940s snapshot
the roots of family struggle to yield
shoots. It's a photo I've not seen before:
sunny day, someone's tree-filled backyard.
Dad is maybe seventeen; my mother,
corsage pinned to her jacket, stands next to him
but arm-in-arm with her best girlfriend,
not with this freckled redhead who
discovered her in third-period French class.

Is she ambivalent, or just shy? His
expression is noncommittal, unreadable.
He and the other boy in the foursome
are wearing suits, this clearly a double date.
My parents' inscrutable faces haunt me;
I want to shake them out of their neutrality.
You two, I want to tell them—you're perfect
together; hurry up and fall in love. Life
won't be as long as you might think.

Wendy McVicker

Anger, Waiting

A day gone wrong,
that started out just fine.
Wind, sun, clouds jamming
in a blue–gray corner
of the sky.
We took a walk,
drank coffee in our favorite
café, passed the paper
back and forth.
Then a jolt, like bitter
when you expect sweet.
And we don't know
each other anymore.

A door opens, sudden,
blowing dank air
in your face

and you know
you have to enter,
you have to start
down those stairs
and find what breathes
in the shadows, what creature
reaches out, what it holds
in its twisted fist—

what it wants you
to have

Karen Whittington Nelson

Center

At the center of my life
I am but water and air—
a soft rain quenching
a garden of thirst,
evaporating into the ether
after a storm.
A blind spot on a fogged lens,
invisible
beyond these hills and trees.
A hidden spring, a bubbling joy,
holding my breath against
icy hail
and windfall sorrow.

Mischelle Anthony

Cling

Summer slouches away at the keyboard,
putters down the path.

Of course, mosquitos and sweat,
the world darkening between
Crisco eyelids once olive oil.

A sugar ant plunges forehead
to collar bone, some anthill
imagining its way beneath the skull.

Another one clears a shoulder blade.

Yesterday my friend hid from a fish
head's grin along the levy macadam,
flies in its gathering stink.

She clung to my right arm,
moaned *Ohhhh, no* to escape
its circle of an eye, the triangle
luminescent, grey, fins a memory
beneath the lowering sky.

When gnats settle on neck, forearm,
and ankle bone, you have to
wonder if it's enough.

The birch out back leafs every April
even as the bark peels away
from its trunk, a wooden shore.

Ellen Austin-Li

The Curtain

Bobby lost both legs below the knee,
torched when he passed out, in his bed,
dead drunk, with a lit cigarette.
I was his nurse that night he came back
to the unit, post-allograft—skin placed
on his stumps to cut down on infection.
Already septic, he was hallucinating, loopy
inside the BCNU, the plastic tent that kept him
in high heat and humidity & kept out the germs
that threaten big burns. Post-op, he shook
in rhythm with the rigors of fever, his eyes wild
& following me as I moved around the bedside,
reaching inside with gauntlets, masked and gowned,
fiddling with IV lines. Earlier, I heard report
from Anita, who told me where the skin had come
from. The donor: Bobby's Dad. Dead
from an MI the day before. Bobby didn't know.
His mind deemed too far gone
in the world of febrile dreams to glean
with all that was going on. Bobby grabbed
my arm hard as it passed over his face.
He's right there, he's right there, he rasped.
I held his eyes and replied: *There's no one
here, Bobby, it's just me and you—
back from the OR—you're seeing things.
I'm your nurse, you were burned,
Remember?* But he wouldn't let go,
digging in, hissing, insisting I listen.
Get him off me, get him off me, he chanted,

frantic, eyes flares of panic. He pointed
at the foot of the bed. The curtain shimmered
where he gestured, hovering over his bandaged legs.
He's right there, Bobby whispered, *can't you see
him? My father! He's right there!*
A chill entered when I realized—
We were not alone.

KB Ballentine

When We Get There, I Will Have Nothing Left to Tell

May's promise shaved by rain and chill,
this unexpected bite another reminder
we are not in control.
407 days sequestered left us hovering
our doorways, hesitating between safe solitude
and living.

Drawings of masks graffiti store doors,
burden us with more decisions
than what to buy—
now it's a matter of cost.
We saunter the sidewalks but still turn away
from others passing by, dogs and children skittish.
We no longer smile or say hello—
our very breath germinating the air.

We squint in the light, expect the world
to be changed and instead find ourselves
altered.
Unlike Birds of Paradise, we have languished
without sun, without benefit of anything
except rootedness
which we have clutched—exercising
our right to silence, to darkness.
Wondering why there is no song.

Victoria Woolf Bailey
The Secret Life of Parents

We are like wild animals,
making love in the rain,
thunder and the smell of
burning oak.

We show you the world,
the world we want you to see,
reading the newspaper,
drinking tea.

Jim Minick

Spring Dance

Digital Photography

Elissa Yancey
Modern Mother Love

1.

Mother love didn't come naturally to me. Aching and sore from 72 hours of wide-awake labor and last-minute incisions, I tensed when my demanding first baby turned his deep blue eyes toward mine. My mind raced. What if I couldn't feed him enough? What were those horrible cramps? What if he didn't latch on? When would I stop bleeding?

As Nicholas marked a half-year out of the womb, I turned 30 and lingered in postpartum depression. I struggled to find a new rhythm with a baby who fought sleep; I cursed the fact that he couldn't tell me what he needed. My three-year-old marriage began to fray under the pressure of sleepless nights and my slow healing. The thought of having sex after months of perineal pain terrified me. I imagined my stitches ripping apart, our bed damp with blood. Everywhere I turned, I was letting the people I loved most down in fundamental ways. My life was not going as planned.

I grew up near Cincinnati, Ohio, in a working-class family, convinced that a fulfilling life looked like a straight line—an upward path of mobility that could be accessible by working hard and playing by the rules. I remember the first time I saw a cartoon comparing how we expect our life's journey to look versus the reality of it. It consists of two square boxes, side by side: the box on the left shows a straight line, inching upward—a solid-stroke of progress extending from the tip of an arrow. The box on the right, on the other hand, offers a hot mess of squiggles and curves, circles and tremors that crawl right then jerk left, drift up and plummet down. While messy and chaotic, the box on the right, the caption points out, is the realistic, and richer, route. Embrace the squiggles, the explanation goes, for they hold both adventure and wisdom. But when I looked at the squiggles, I saw the line art equivalent of despair. That might hold value for other people, I thought, but not for me.

As the youngest of six kids, I was pure left-box material. I was the tail end of the first generation of my family to earn four-year degrees. I got a full scholarship to a local public university; I excelled along my privileged path. I worked both in and out of school, determined to save enough money not only to pay for an apartment and car but also to travel and see the world. After graduating, I spent three months backpacking through Europe with a friend. When I returned home with a new appreciation for education, I earned a fellowship at a private university for graduate school. My life was a left-box success story.

I fell in love with and married a talented and funny product designer. I was proud to work, whether it was as a teacher or a temp, to pay my half of our bills. My life trajectory remained unshaken by personal tragedy or loss. Whenever I felt challenged or underestimated, I was sustained by my mom's oft-repeated mantra: "No one is better than you; and you're not better than anybody."

She reassured me with the first half of that motto during my initial days home after delivering my son. The days when I began to feel the first tremors disrupting the dependable straightness of my dependable lifeline. She sat across from my bed, holding my newborn when my arms grew shaky; she hummed happy, nameless tunes to soothe us both. She made sure that I drank enough water and that my baby's cries didn't interrupt my daytime naps.

Still, a part of me resisted soothing. I tended toward irrational thinking, convinced I was an inadequate mother and focused on my new uncertainty as a threatening squiggle in the line of my life. When Nicholas resisted rest and I couldn't find a book my mom had used to lull me to sleep as a child, I called her in a crying panic. She urged patience. "Wait a few months," she said. "He's too young to appreciate it, anyway." Sure enough, I tracked down a copy a few months later. Unfortunately, my son found its droopy-eyed characters and sing-songy rhymes more funny than sleep-inducing.

The joy of introducing solid foods to my genuinely happy baby soured when, after he nibbled with interest on scrambled eggs, his whole body convulsed and became covered with hives. His severe food allergies, to eggs and then to peanuts, brought a new wave of tremors to our house. Neither his father nor I had any food allergies, so every meal came with a side of the unknown. The fear of catastrophe, in the shape of a single peanut or egg noodle, inspired my next phase of near-manic motherhood. I judged every situation by its potential allergen risk, overplanning playdates and buying bulk snacks free of peanuts or eggs so that my son never felt left out. By sheer force of will, I thought I could iron out these squiggles and keep my family safe.

When I got pregnant again, I asked our allergist the odds for a second child having the same allergies. "50/50," she replied. I did not laugh. My second child, Owen, had his first allergic reaction—to egg—on his first birthday.

I scoured ingredient lists and joined national groups for parents of kids with severe food allergies as squiggles reshaped my path. When Nicholas started preschool, I trained everyone in the school how to use an EpiPen; I chaperoned every field trip.

In our small family, I served as doctor-mom—the parent

in charge of giving medicines, delivering breathing treatments during Nicholas' all-night asthma bouts and watching with a practiced if inauthentic calm through every food allergy scare. It was a mothering duty that felt both stressful and necessary; I felt the anxiety I hid from my sons settle somewhere beneath my chest. At night, I could feel it underneath my ribs, a pulsing seismograph of uncertainty.

As much as I loved my sons, I was done with babies. I felt helpless in a life so far from my straight-line expectations. When a dad in our friend group reported his relief after his vasectomy, I asked my husband what he thought of the idea. He paused, but only briefly. He recalled our sons' births and their impact on my body. He said a vasectomy seemed like an opportunity for him to do something in return. Yes, he'd do it. The gnawing tremors in my core calmed. I had never loved him more.

2.

A squiggle is a doodle of despair. It curls and loops in an irregular way, its continuous line twisting, turning, shifting upward and down, back and forth, creating chaos.

Yet in modern art, a squiggle carries weight and meaning. It defines space, it creates moods, it builds worlds of inclusion and exclusion. It has taken me years of museum visits to recognize, much less engage with, what I used to see as the simplistic strokes that define the walls of contemporary art wings. Art that defied realism; art that conjured other complex expressions of life; art that forced a reckoning–of self and other.

Far from random, these squiggles carry narratives that bend our thinking and twist our perceptions. Their intentionality sparks a struggle in sense-making that is both visceral and intellectual.

Consider work by American abstract expressionist

Lee Krasner, whose vast knowledge of art made her a force both in and out of her studio, before, during and after her marriage to Jackson Pollock. Her 1962 lithograph, *Obisdian*, offers a boundary-pushing path through a forest of emotion with squiggles that trace and simultaneously hold a sense of belonging, a sense of extending and a sense of loss.

3.

It was a sunny summer day when my dad suffered his fatal heart attack, more than a dozen healthy years after his first. He had started the day early, enjoying a round of golf with friends. My mom had been at my house while he played, watching my sons, almost three and almost one, as I got a haircut. I remember my dad picking her up and, in an unusual display of affection, him hugging me goodbye. Within an hour, he was brain dead.

In the wake of my dad's death, I became obsessed with the irrational notion that my mom was going to die at any moment. I found it hard to sleep. In nightmares, I rushed to her house, shoeless, to find she had disappeared. Whenever she didn't answer her phone, I'd drop whatever was happening in my own life and drive to her house, heart pounding, worried I would find her collapsed on the living room floor, just like my dad.

Those drives to my mom's house, 15 minutes each way, always speeding, took time and attention away from my husband and my sons. After a speeding ticket that was hard to rationalize, I asked one of my mom's neighbors to keep an eye out and call me if they saw any cause for worry. Then, when they called to say my mom had nearly run over a child on a tricycle at the end of her driveway, I realized my worst fears were not even worst-case scenarios. Begrudgingly and all at once, both she and I realized that our days of independence were over.

Our relationship shaped my days, and friction with my husband grew. I watched over my mom's check-writing and bill management; I took her to her doctors and the grocery. We still had fun when possible, like during trips to Value City and thrift stores, where bargains were as abundant as our joy at finding them and the ride home always included a stop at a drive-thru for a Frosty. As long as my sons were too young to protest, I brought them along to spend time at her house while I checked on her; most days, they were a balm to her. But as our roles reversed, her frustration at being dependent grew. When her temper sharpened and flared, so did my resentment. Our twisted lines overlapped in unnatural contortions.

4.

The contrasts are stark in the forceful lines of Lee Krasner's *Rising Green*, a mammoth work of abstract expressionism she completed in 1972. It was 10 years after she nearly died from a brain aneurysm; years when she embraced nature and Matisse. Nearly seven feet tall and almost six feet wide, *Rising Green* is bold and declarative in white and black, green and pink: bird and feather; leaf and flower bud. Its intentional figures caress two sides of the painting and reach beyond the others; a dynamic portrayal of what can—and cannot—be contained by art.

With sharp angles and swooping curves, it is bisected by a single spear-like shaft of green — the only straight line as a statement that connects and divides. It shapes stork and flamingo; it balances geometry and poetry. A vibrant vision of nature, the painting shifts a degree, offsets an angle and leaves brushstrokes reaching toward one another. The yearning is palpable, the consummation always just out of reach.

5.

My husband and I joked about the lame Musak in the waiting room at the urologist's office. A 1970s relic of a space, the room's beiges and browns felt more outdated than comforting. There were only three other people in the room, all men, and we were all spaced conspicuously far apart, self-selecting privacy with distance and lowered eyes. I patted my husband's hand and leaned toward him, a physical offering of support. When he pulled his hand away, he spoke nervously and twisted the arm on his glasses. "What if you die and I meet another woman and want to have kids with her?" he asked. "What if one of our kids dies? Won't we want to have another baby to replace him?" he kept going, his voice a sharp whisper. "I've read some awful stories on the internet about permanent pain after vasectomies."

I tried to reassure him. Finally, I took his hand and said we could walk out the door at that moment if he wasn't sure of his decision. It was his choice. He demurred. "Are you serious?" he asked. I answered in the affirmative. "It's too late now, though," he countered. Then a nurse called his name and he headed back for the procedure.

A full year passed before his constant pelvic pain started in earnest, but he always traced it back to that day, that office, that procedure. He was plagued with infections that could never be precisely identified or completely cured. Lower-body pain spread to his back and intensified; sitting, which he did for work, became torture and pain pills became essential. Based on doctors I sourced and interviewed, we flew from Ohio to Johns Hopkins in Baltimore and drove 11-plus hours to the Mayo Clinic in Minnesota, our toddler sons in tow. His pain persisted, and his anger toward me grew.

I found refuge in work. I'd taken a job at the city

magazine for the steady paycheck and health insurance after my husband stopped working altogether because of his chronic pain. But I grew to love the career I was building. At work, I could still present a picture-perfect family life—all straight lines and forward progress. I socialized with people who never glimpsed my fissures, people who never looked closely enough to see the tremors just below the surface.

My colleagues didn't know when I slipped out to pick up Owen after morning preschool and tucked him at my feet under my desk, arranging his backpack with his coat thrown over it as a pillow so he could nap while I worked. They never suspected the closed-door phone fights with my husband that happened most mornings or saw my reddened eyes before I patted them clear with damp paper towels from the bathroom down the hall. Or the maze of emotional scars his repeated accusations left behind, scars that retraced my weaknesses, fears and failures. They cut deep and raw: he had only gotten a vasectomy because I had demanded it. My selfishness had ruined his life. Now no other woman would want him. I didn't deserve him.

I was grateful my co-workers couldn't also distinguish phone interviews from my multiple daily calls to my mom. First, I'd ask about what medicines she had or hadn't taken, what food she had or hadn't eaten, what exercise she had or hadn't yet completed. Then our roles re-jumbled into their natural order, and I could confess to the tremors shaking my steady-seeming life.

My let-down list was long: I had left my sons stranded in their elementary school office for more than an hour after their father, in a medicated haze mixed with depression, slept through multiple alarms. I had limited their out-of-school activities because I ran out of time, patience and money to juggle carpools and safe-snack duties. I had become a "because

I said so" mom with a short fuse and few explanations.

Still, every time I shared my shaky ground, my mom granted me absolution and relentless understanding. She told me she was proud of me and insisted that my accomplishments left her in awe. She acknowledged the twists and turns that had upended my life expectations, then pointed out the growth she saw in me because of them. She kneaded each squiggle like a tight muscle until I relaxed into its strength.

6.

Lee Krasner painted *Gaea* in 1966, the year after I was born and a full decade after her famous husband's death. Its squiggles are central to the massive work's emotional wealth. The piece, a modern expression of the ancient Greek earth goddess, flows and somersaults in black and red, secure in its strength as well as the varying weight of its curves and lines. Some thick and lip-like, others thin and jagged, these squiggles gesture with intent.

Looking at the fullness of *Gaea*, I see Krasner, whose intellect pushed her more famous partner further into his genius, whose appreciation for his mind allowed her to fight for his sobriety and creative freedom. She eschewed mothering a child with Pollock, the love of her life, not out of an aversion to being a parent, but out of respect for its all-consuming nature. Already maternal to Pollock, she understood that another life dependent on her guidance and support would destroy her.

In one glance at *Gaea*, I see feathers and eggs floating in and out of focus. They are surrounded by splattered curves; they are vulnerable, resting softly in an open hand. They emerge from shadows, at once essential and dangerous. I look again and see traces of human faces and figures leaning left and right; they are in conversation and alone; they are exploring and grounded. They are nature at her messy, voluptuous best.

Sam Barbee

The Wake

My birth mother, Barbara,
never *finished schoolin*,
was always *a hard workin gal*.
Grounded by slight square-footage.

Before today, she always kept
a bright face, modest halo
around bright blue eyes.
Her older-sister Vera Mae has died.

Easy to ignore the mountain sky–
clouds seal bare autumn peaks
visible from her Mt. Airy porch.
Wail without echo. Her almanac

confirms an overcast afternoon.
In the living room, a few
of my half-sisters vigil
around her TV chair.

All hands open to comfort
while Barbara cradles a family Bible
across her knees. Face droops
to a new page. One palm

holds an unframed B&W photo
of *Mae and Me*. Feet on a stool,
chin to her chest, slow-paced
sorrow prods. A woman

of few mirrors, cannot recognize
a reflection. Having always lived
content with solemn acceptance,
      discloses *I can't be eased.*

Rhonda Pettit

Glass Negative

They don't smile. They don't hold a pose
in 1903 they can't keep forever or can take
lightly. They look ahead, beyond themselves and us,
above the glass negative that will put them

in place—*here!*—like a Darwin specimen. Exposure
draws them out, the shutter drops. All we will see:
Respectable Gibson Girl
Perfect Gentleman

not the farmer with corn along the Licking,
tobacco rising to crown a stony ridge; not
the farm wife saving scraps of all kinds—slop
for hogs, cloth for quilts, poems for sweetness—

humming hymns while making rhubarb pie
or tending wild roses; not the four children
making them wish for more; not a future
etched by depression and war no chemistry

can leave in black and white this day. When held
up to light, what else did it fail to capture
their dark shapes could not begin
to picture?

Reduced to image and expanded in range,
Albert and Alpharetta will light upon other
hands, frames, shelves, distant speculations—
then fade
               long after the glass negative
shatters into stars on the floor.

Roy Bentley
"Hey, That's No Way to Say Goodbye"
—*Leonard Cohen*

I was 25 when a friend said, Lose the sunglasses at night.
Gradient tinted wire-rims like ones John Lennon sported.

I may have told him to fuck himself, but I heard him out.
In this life, you don't want to be an ass. Or listen to one.

A bully of a kind men know. Women, too. Reminded me,
then, of that mistral-Suzanne in the song: he made tea and

shared a variety of orange come all the way from China,
but he acted like his presence was a gift or, for you, lucky.

In his defense, we were the same age; though I was married,
and so I couldn't roam nightlife-streets in our college town.

This was nineteen seventy-nine. Jimmy Carter was president.
Me and this guy were friends. And friends will presume shit

about you. Maybe he was busting balls, as they used to say;
and maybe I never cared that much for the company of men.

I can't blame him for thinking that he could hand me advice:
he was from Cleveland, which knows it's tougher than the rest

of the brokenhearted rust-belt cities of the American Midwest.
Oh: and he said he flushed my self-published book of poetry

down his American Standard toilet. Said it like he'd done me
a great kindness—which, now that I think of it, maybe he had.

Marc Harshman

The Secrets of Family Life

> *This hour I tell things in confidence,*
> *I might not tell everybody, but I will tell you.*
> —Walt Whitman

He slides down the hill on his ass.
His dog started it, and he had grown
to envy her such little pleasures.
The girl he lives with, Nancy, has orange hair
          and wears moccasins beaded with bright
              green and plum plastic.
She never knows the time of day
          and he likes her most for that.
She works in the city and speaks Swedish
          with her parents who live on the phone….
well, somewhere, anyway—they do not live here.
He's kept the mirror his mother gave him.
It sits on the mantle and, though inconvenient,
          he wanders back and forth from the bathroom
            to shave before it.
Nancy has never seemed to notice:
          another admirable quality.
But the ass-sliding down the lawn in back of their flat, that
          he keeps for Sundays
while she's at Mass, or mid-afternoons
          before she returns from the city.
Nancy needs to get to know the dog better,
          he thinks, before she can be let in
on the little secrets of family life.

Dan Leach
Lockjaw

We're building a ramp in the cut between our trailers. The wood we stole from the construction site doesn't match the wood we stole from school, but we don't care. It's summer and we're building something, me swinging the hammer, Tiny holding the nails.

"What's lockjaw?" Tiny asks, after we've finished and are deciding where to steal some paint.

"Who you been talking to?" I say, using a voice I learned from a late-night movie where one guy throws a knife straight into another guy's forehead.

"My mom," he says, using his real voice, which wouldn't scare a hamster.

"You tell her about the house too?"

"Hell no," says Tiny, all scared now, shaking his head from side to side and making me think I should get all my voices from the things I watch at night.

"Then why was your mom talking about lockjaw?"

"Found a nail in my shoe."

"What are you doing with a nail in your shoe?"

"It was an accident. From yesterday, when we went to the house."

"Oh," I say, in my normal, non-movie voice.

"So what is it?"

"It's when you step on something rusty and get infected. Does something to your blood and makes it so you can't move your mouth."

I flex my jaw to show him. "Like this," I say, through gnashed teeth.

Tiny makes his mouth like mine. Mutters "Really?"

Bright blue eyes full of bright blue fear, he winces.

"Damn," he says and, releasing, rubs his throat. "Sounds awful."

"I've heard of worse," I say and, in some ways, am not lying.

"I haven't," says Tiny.

"Better watch out, then," I tell him, nudging the hammer against his sternum. "Better watch where you walk."

We hide the ramp and head to my house. We ditch our bikes in the yard and try to slip into the kitchen without my mother noticing. She does though and gets off the couch to interrogate Tiny.

"Where y'all going?" she says, fist on her hip, all pretending for his sake. Tiny knows better than to lie to my mother. Sober, she can spot a lie regardless of what smoke it's wrapped in. Today, though, she's a far sight from sober. But since Tiny's too young to read eyes or figure what's in someone's cup, he stays scared and says nothing. Just chews on that bee-stung bottom lip that makes people in our trailer park ask who his father is.

"I said where y'all going?" she repeats, phantom tough because she too has seen her share of movies.

Shooting Tiny a "Watch this" wink, I step in between them and looking her dead in her watery eyes say, "They're about to play ghost tag down in the cul-de-sac."

"Alright then," she says and looks around the living room for her cigarettes. "Y'all be safe."

With her back on the couch, we grab what we need from the pantry and bust out the back door. While walking towards our bikes, I reach my hand down into my pocket. Even though I know it's there, I like to touch my Swiss Army knife.

Something about cold, hard metal sitting in your hand and feeling like a promise.

Outside, Tiny spits through his teeth like I taught him and says, "That was close."

"Don't worry, man. I got your back," I say, which is something else I got from that movie with the knife-throwing hero.

"And I have yours too," says Tiny. "We're not late, are we?"

"Come on," I say, and ride towards the construction site, Tiny breathing hard behind me.

We use the binoculars to make sure he's still there. The grass around the construction site is gold and overgrown and, except for the house he's in, there's no buildings around. Of course, he's there: right where we left him yesterday, slumped on that half-built porch with his empty cans of beer and Glad-bag full of nothings.

For Tiny's sake, I scan the ground for anything with a nail sticking out of it.

"Do you see him?" Tiny asks.

"To the East," I say, nodding towards the backside of the development.

I say *East* and Tiny looks impressed, but I've been turned around ever since Miss Torwalt taught us moss only grows on the North side of trees and the sun sets in the West. I doubt Miss Torwalt has ever been to our trailer park, where the trees have moss on all sides and the sun goes down a different place each night.

We share the binoculars. From back on the ridge, the bum doesn't look like much. It's when we get right up on him that we see the hair like bleach-white seaweed stretched over his scalp. We see the pink skin splotched with mud-colored freckles. Right up on him, we see the red eyes. *Albino* was the word the encyclopedia gave to it and since I looked at plenty of pictures the night before I'm not half as scared as Tiny, who has no choice but to fear the unfamiliar since his mom can't afford decent literature.

"Bring it here," barks the bum, standing up when we're still twenty feet away.

Tiny falls in behind me, and I'm waiting to feel a tug on my shirt the way he used to when we'd sneak into Old Man Frazier's junkyard and mess with his goat, or when we'd climb on Miss Jameson's grill to peek into her bathroom window. He used to twist the ends of my shirts into little handles for him to hold onto and when things got bad it felt like I was dragging him. He doesn't grab it, though, and I'm tempted to turn around and let him know I 'm proud of how far he's come. "Courage comes in degrees," was something my father used to say, and I see the point is not without its application.

Ten feet out the bum charges us. Tiny grabs me. I grab the knife inside my pocket. The backpack with the food falls to the ground.

"Relax," the bum says, snatching the backpack off the ground and returning to his spot on the porch. Fingers wrapped around the knife, I imagine throwing it, picking as my target a large beige mole on his neck. I envision the blade leaving my hand and sliding, like a coin into a slot, into his flesh.

"Where's the magazine?" says Tiny.

"About that," he says and tells us a story about getting rolled.

Watching his brown mouth deliver the story, I think about what my father used to say about excuses, about how they're like assholes because everybody has them and they always stink. If I didn't care about being original, I would've repeated his saying word for word. But Tiny's spent too much time around my father and I'm trying to teach him to find his own voice. It doesn't do to spend your whole life repackaging other people's best riffs.

So what I say is, "We held up our end of the deal," then look back to make sure Tiny's good. And he is.

"You little pervs will get your mag. Just need more time is all."

Tiny sniffs the air loud enough for us all to notice and then, after hesitating for a moment, says, "Y'all smell that?"

In unison, the bum and I inhale, attempting to catch the scent in question. But before either of us can process the alleged scent, Tiny sneers and says, "Smells like bullshit to me." Out shoots my palm. Tiny slaps it. *By degrees, Old Son.*

"I know," the bum says and looks halfway sincere in his shame. "And I'm sorry."

"When then?" says Tiny, still talking with his new gall and largeness.

"Day after tomorrow. Swear I'll have it."

He sticks out his filthy hand in Tiny's direction. Tiny though, instead of shaking it, turns on his heel and says over his shoulder, "Damn right you will."

I don't let go of the knife until we're back up on the ridge and peddling towards home. Every so often I turn around to make sure Tiny is behind me. And he is.

Back home, Tiny asks if I can come over. His mother is fixing breakfast-for-supper, which means scrambling eggs and soaking blueberry muffins in melted butter before dropping them in the Fry Daddy.

"I'm game," I say. "And given the task at hand, we might as well make it a sleepover."

When Tiny looks confused, I spell it out for him: how we'll sneak out and go back to the house; how we'll see firsthand what the bum is hiding in his trash-bag; how if we don't return with our magazine, we'll damn sure find something to tip the scales back to our side.

Tiny says nothing after this. Just nods his head, bites his lip. Whatever he had back the construction site is gone, ditched at the door like our muddy shoes.

"What?" I say. "Are you scared that we're going to get caught?"

Tiny nods.

"Listen," I say, knife-thrower's voice in full effect. "That bum couldn't catch a cold."

Miracle of miracles: the line, my father's, works. Out shoots Tiny's hand. I slap it and for some reason, repeat the line. "That bum couldn't catch a cold."

We laugh.

Later, after Tiny's mother has passed out, we slip out the back door and ride down to the ridge. Thirty feet back is a streetlamp, but its light doesn't reach the construction site. The darkness below us is different than the one behind us. And we know it. Crouched down and saying nothing, we both silently consider the best way to go home without seeming like a coward. We know from the movies what happens to cowards.

"How do we know he's down there?" whispers Tiny, his face so close to mine that I can smell the blueberries on his breath.

"Where else is he gonna go?" I whisper back and, because it seems like the right thing to do, reach into my pocket and pull out the Swiss Army knife.

"Here," I say and lay it in Tiny's hand. "Just in case."

"Okay," he says and holds it in his hand like a wounded bird.

Tiny flicks out the large blade. What few stars still hang above us make it shine like the straight white teeth of a familiar smile. I watch Tiny rub his thumb along the edge. I watch him snap it back in place and stand up taller than before.

"Don't worry," I whisper, leading the way down the hill. "We'll be back before you know it."

Yesterday's rain has left the mud just wet enough to give off a sharp smacking sound as we tiptoe to the edge of the porch. Our steps stick, not enough to lose a shoe, but enough to slow us down and make some noise. He's snoring as a drunk will, but still we stop every so often to make sure he's going steady. And he is. Steady drunk and sleeping right beside the bag.

I'm knifeless but carrying a dollar store flashlight. Tiny's right behind me, twisting the bottom of my shirt into a handle. His hand is trembling. I almost tell him to go wait for me on the ridge. Then I remember the Swiss Army knife and say nothing. I take the step in front of me and conjure a vision of Tiny, courage complete, spinning through the air and gutting the bum. Old Tiny, bad as a late-night movie.

My mind's eye is on fire with Tiny's victory when the plank beneath my foot lets out a moan so loud my thumb twitches and actually flicks on the light. Paralyzed, we watch as a beam of light finds and frames the bum's face. Tiny lets out a whimper and flings himself off the porch. I begin to backpedal, but by some sick trick of gravity the light stays trained on the face and, falling backwards, I am forced to watch his eyes like two tiny flaming discs snap open. Tiny screams, and I drop the flashlight, and the bum rises to his feet, and we turn to run, and I am gone. Tiny is screaming, and I am gone. In all that vile darkness behind me, the smack of mud and muffled voices blend, but I do not know what is happening. I do not know a thing. Screaming fills my ears, and I am gone, gone, gone.

I run through the dark until I'm home, and the door's locked, and I am looking at my mother's face, bathed as it is in the blue glow of the television. I am nearly crying when I wake her.

"What?" says my mother, sitting up and rubbing her eyes. "What is it?"

"I had a bad dream," I lie and collapse into her outstretched arms.

By the time I collect myself and go to the window that looks out on Tiny's house, his porch light is on, but his bike is nowhere I can see. I think about going back out, at least to check his house if not to return to the construction site. And I'm on the verge of doing so before my mother calls me into the living room and starts firing off questions about what happened. It's just sweet tea in her cup tonight so it takes a good half hour to set her straight.

By the time I return to the window, Tiny's bike is lying on his lawn.

I don't dream that night because I don't sleep. It's those eyes that keep me up. The eyes and the screams. I imagine the knife-throwing hero is standing watch by my window, and I catch a quick nap before morning.

The next morning, I go over to Tiny's house. His mother opens the door. Her smile says she doesn't know. Then she tells me he's in his room. When I open his door, Tiny's still in bed, staring up at the ceiling where he has stuck about a dozen of those glow-in-the-dark stars in the shape of a smiley face. He does not look away from the stars when I come in.

"Hey buddy," I say and pat the bottom of his foot.

"Hey," Tiny says, quiet but distant, like an echo down a hall or a voice from one room over.

"Last night was kind of wild," I say and sit on the edge of the bed.

"Yep," Tiny says, louder but still distant, still faded and far off sounding.

He still hasn't looked at me. His body is stiff, arms arranged straight down along his sides, legs unbent and neatly outstretched. His mouth has a tight quality and as I notice these things, I begin to think about the time between me getting home and me seeing Tiny's bike. I look around the room for the Swiss Army knife and see no sign of it. I can't bring myself to ask him about it.

Instead, I say, "That old bum chase you very far?"

"Nope," whimpers Tiny and shakes his head from side to side.

"So you got away clean, huh?" I say, forcing a laugh.

Tiny doesn't answer right away. He opens his mouth as if he means to say one thing, but then, as if something catches the words before he can release them, says nothing. Just swallows hard. Finally, with that small unmoving mouth, he whispers, "Yep."

When it becomes clear Tiny isn't going to say anything else, I get up.

"See you around, then," I say and hold out my hand for him to slap.

He doesn't, though. He stares at the stars on his ceiling and no longer seems to know that I'm in the room. Just lays there and breathes. And then I'm not in the room. I'm outside, walking towards my house and thinking of what the knife-thrower would say. But the best movie line I come up with isn't good enough. Not even close.

Pam Campbell
Until Death Do Us

part...you didn't say it,
my new father-in-law insisted, popping
peanuts handful after handful, pulverizing,
open-mouthed. Tossed and turned
by tongue and teeth, his muddied
saliva bit and chewed my marriage day.
Until death do us part...you didn't say it.

His son and I memorized our marriage vows:
more meaningful, more personal,
more binding, so I thought.
I take you
to be my husband,
to have and to hold, not own
from this day forward.

The night before warned:
His *god-damn, fucking idiot* rained hard
when I, knees down in midnight grass, refused
to stop searching
for the tiny, gold cross necklace
precious to one unused to gifts.
I ran but returned, priest-calmed

for better, for worse,
binding, sentence,
for richer, for poorer,
I, accustomed to lean days, didn't fear this,
but he, figures-possessed and stranger

to how sides burn and ache
with only one meal a day, did.

in sickness and in health, a one-sided trade
to love and to cherish, the hardest casualty
till death us do part. I did say it
This is my solemn vow. I kept my promise
even when blue-black nights,
fogged mornings drilled
a one-sided covenant.

KENNETH CHAMLEE

Dark Edge

Why not, I thought, the wind being calm and the afternoon
pale as my son's hair, so I said Yes, you can go
with the men of Lake Jeanette Fishing Club
who give two-dollar rides on a Sunday afternoon,
swinging orange-vested toddlers into johnboats
and electric-motored canoes.

The boats scattered into zigzags, beelines and curves,
each captain styling the trip to his craft, and off went my son
zippered into a high-visibility preserver hugging his coil of ribs.
I was thinking I hadn't asked the skipper's name or even
gotten a good look at his face under that tugged-down ball cap
as the boat puttered into a far cove and disappeared.

How long is long enough? One minute? Three minutes? Five?
On the dock of a small lake not four miles from our house
I listened to a toolbox of dads saw up yesterday's scores and believed
the planks were buckling under me like untendoned bones.
Most thoughts slip like leaves down a spillway but some
catch a dark edge and eddy forever.   When the boat reappeared
my son waved like a flame in a signal torch.
As I grabbed him off the dock he pitched back,
stiff-arming us into a capital Y, shrilling Guess what we saw?!
I touched his chattering mouth, watched the boatman lift
another child, and thought, okay, it's all right, nothing
happened, and
what, what was I thinking?

Hilda Downer

The Arrow

When I asked Wiley what was the worst thing he has ever done,
his answer was handy.
When I was a young'un,
I shot my Granny in the butt with an arrow.
I asked if she got mad.
Nah, she was hanging out clothes
knew I was just playing,
and didn't mean it.
Even the worst thing Wiley has done is funny.

That isn't true for everyone.
I think of another Granny when I was growing up—
God-fearing and so good
that you became good around her.
Before she and her husband wed,
she became pregnant.
For that one thing,
she lived her life with the undertow of shame.

Shame is a kind of missing
who we would have been without it.
It rusts from the inside out.
Wiley had the ability not to regret,
not to miss.

Zen Buddhist monks never missed—
so proficient at hitting the target.
Not to waste arrows during practice,
they simply pulled back on the empty bow.

Published in *Wiley's Last Resort*. Hickory: Redhawk Publications, 2022.

NATALIE KIMBELL

On the Pound Near Phillips Creek in Virginia

I couldn't sleep, visiting Grandma near Phillips Creek.
Barefoot on thin cold linoleum floors
so peeled in places that hand-hewn wood
peered up through worn peony patterns.

The mold of earth and time threaded air,
disturbed only by the sooty smoke and crack
of coal burning. The fireplace hissed and popped.
Ghost shadows licked walls and dark ceilings,

But I, hypnotized by voices in hushed tones,
edged on, wanting to be a part of them. The comradery
of women after work stops. The music of mothers
whispering on the Pound on Phillips Creek in Virginia.

Closer I drew, but out of sight, I huddled
nightgown over my knees in the darkened
hall between the pie safe and kitchen.
Hiding, pressed against the paneled wall,

I nestled there chilling on the floor, listening
to names muted in turbulence. My grandmother spoke
her brother's name, who passed the winter before.
Her speech heated, unleashed on his ex-wife, Silvania.

Why she witched him! His money was what she wanted
my Grandma hurled. *She caught her cum and laced his drink.*
No man can resist the wilds of a witch. And with a spit,
thrown words lodged inside my head.

Fifteen years later, as a teacher of teens,
I blushed when words were being thrown
between girls in a bombardment of sexual slurs,
when a word hit the centrifuge of memory.

In an instant, there with chilled understanding,
I huddled again in damp air and coal smoke
listening to the words from the mouths of mothers
on the banks of Phillips Creek on the Pound in Virginia.

Pamela Hirschler
After the Flood

Muddy water still cascades down the mountain,
a froth of current eddies and pulls at the bank,
plastic bottles snag in the bend, a highchair
dangles from an oak with toilet-paper branches.

How many bags will volunteers haul away,
how many cans will be traded for change,
how many families won't worry about river trash
when they shovel mud from their living rooms?

But the bloodroot and bluebells still emerge,
the redbud blooms, and the wren twitters at its mate,
pushes a tattered drinking straw into the nest,
and with a thin bill, weaves it home.

You can know a place
by what the flood leaves behind.

Michael Dowdy

When I Shop, I Dream of Rivers of Workers Building a Dam

We settlers kept it simple
when we coined the waters.
Here a New, there a Back.
The Big Stony rushes down
to its Little sibling. Creeks
don't hold grudges, deny
nutrients, seek revenge
against the lower streams.

Consider Poverty or Sinking.
Each empties its burdens,
settlers who knew better
called their gallons, into
the New. Are these creeks
mirrors of want and will?
Or white jets of mercy
and its cousin damnation?

Consider Tom's and John's.
Consider seeing Strouble's
with outsider ears. No local
would rhyme the creek
with Double's or Trouble's.
The *true* in Strouble's
takes a languid bend.
Had grown men with scant
ken named these streams?

At the first hint of spring
I wade into these waters
white as Tylenol, the pills
of my toenails burning
in the pebbles. Cleansed
by the current, what name
does the river of my life
receive? The Plumb Wore
Out, the Running Man,
the Skinny Oblivion,
the Tongue-Tied Louse?

Where is the wellspring
of my worth? The fount
from which dollars flow,
becoming more and more
money? The river I wade
into once and again, Capital,
O, Capital, take me down,
guide me to the bank
before I reach the falls.

At this late hour, most
of my brooks and runs
are a trickle, dry as jerky.
One tingles my fingers.
They called it Amazon,
Prime mover of my streams,
the letters into which all
my ones and zeroes flow.

Phyllis Price

Winter Roses

Armed with Daddy's loaded gun,
Mother's feed sack apron,
she married soon—
too many mouths to feed at home.
Her father pulled the man aside—
You watch yourself!

She-wolf fierce about her young
she left them bundled on the bed,
foraged fang and freeze of February
for firewood. Reaching out for kindling
she slipped the embryo,
still too young and imprecise
for memory and regret.

Afterward she lay like prey
until her legs could bear her weight
to walk, not once looking back at steam
risen from frozen ground—
flesh and blood she grieved to leave,
red as winter roses in the snow.

Nettie Farris
Jane

For a while, I wished my name were Jane. People know how to spell it. No discussion required. Not Plain Jane, nor Dick and Jane. But Jane of the first Margaret Drabble novel I ever read: passionate Jane of *The Waterfall,* floating through postpartum delirium. Years later, I imagined myself across from the cash register, saying, "Jane." Then seeing J-A-N-E written on my white cup of dark roast Starbuck's coffee. Jane is a common name and solid. Jane Gray is certainly not solid, she's quite the hot mess, but my connection to her voice strangely anchors me. Still. I have not found the courage to announce my name as anything other than the name written on my birth certificate. I have no idea why. Upon entry to kindergarten, at age five, I insisted that I go by my middle name. For one academic calendar year I was *Elise.* Then I went back to myself no questions asked. I think I was my best, most courageous self at age five. Perfectly anchored in fluidity.

Kari Gunter-Seymour
Legitimate Cockamamie

If I mow the grass today,
it will just need mowing
again next week,
which reminds me,
I need to shave my legs,
though in my defense,
I do believe
I have earned the right
to let my leg hairs grow long.
I should run more,
which reminds me
of my menopause belly,
my body shaming,
the anger and sadness
of my adolescence.
How I let other people
dress me in their dreams,
learned to flaunt scabs
and scars like badges.
Which reminds me
of my grandmother,
her apple breath urging,
live, baby girl, live!
It's not wrong to want,
to follow my fervor,
stand strong in my power,
make mental sculptures
of promises, spray paint
them with graffiti,

drag a ladderback
from the porch,
unwind beneath
the silver maple,
listen for the cold clicks
of creek water,
keep my heart-fire lit
so love can find me.

Jessica Weyer Bentley
Leonard's Juliet

The silver spoons are few.
The empty pews are plenty.
Clutching a peach Nehi on a scorching Cumberland day,
you pray on her fresh grass.
The needle stalked her last vein.
You beseech your Remington,
succumbing to the longing.
A stock boy.
A maid.
A marriage of dearth and whimsy,
charted in the incandescent night,
far above the charred world of slate dumps.

JUDY JENKS

The Diner

Digital Photography
Bristol, Virginia. February 19, 2022.

*Legend has it that this diner is the last place
that Hank Williams was seen alive.*

Preston Martin

Hayride Weather

Mornings pass too quickly,
and the days.

Waning light,
rounds of rain and flurries—
the play of the Gods.

Let's get dizzy
on draughts of bracing air,
the close scent
of stacked bales, burlapped onions,
potato bins.

Let's make to the center
of the cropped field
to better see our blanket
of clouds

and rub the fat belly of the hour.

Ann Thornfield-Long

Whistling the Way Home

  Daddy stood six-foot-four in his bare feet. His brothers, Hershel, Gray, and the youngest, Richard, were all lanky, but Daddy and Richard were the tallest, stood toe-to-toe and saw eye-to-eye on almost everything. They even favored. With their long legs, cowlicks and light eyes, they put me in mind of water birds.

  Daddy was crazy about his baby brother and when he was on the way home from school or work, he would whistle and Uncle Richard would stop what he was doing and run to meet him. Daddy's whistle was like nobody else's; razor sharp, it left a bloodless cut in the air. You could hear Daddy's whistle from one end of Mud Hollow to the other, over two miles away.

  Daddy's family had lived in Mud Hollow for five generations. Most of the men were miners, and some, like Daddy, started out at the mine as boys. It was harder for a tall man to work the mines, Daddy told me. He said you had to start on your knees, like praying, and if you made it to foreman, you had to pray even harder, but you got to do it standing up.

  Before she died of cancer, Daddy's mother made him promise that he would never let Richard work the mine. She'd had a nightmare about it, a cave-in, where everyone got out but Richard. She said Daddy never could lie to her, even when he was little, so it was him she wanted the promise from. Daddy said once he promised her, she let go of his hand and just fell back on her pillows, dead.

  Daddy, Hershel, Gray, and Granddaddy were all working the mine the day Granddaddy had his stroke and lost his mind. Hershel and Janell and their baby moved into Granddaddy's house to care for him, and Uncle Richard moved in with us. Uncle Richard wanted to quit school and go to work in the mines too, but everybody knew Daddy didn't want him there and no one would hire him. Instead, Daddy talked Uncle Richard into finishing school and got him a job butchering at the IGA.

When Daddy and Uncle Richard came home at night, I liked to hang around with them. They were always funny. Sometimes Uncle Richard would put his hands over my ears and turn me around so I couldn't read lips and he'd say something quiet, and Daddy would laugh until he snorted. Then Uncle Richard would laugh harder. He loved to make Daddy snort.

Uncle Richard finally finished school and we all went to his graduation. Daddy dressed up and was so proud. Uncle Richard kept his job at the IGA but the two of them worked on cars on the weekends and sometimes at night down at an old barn about half a mile from the house. The two of them could listen to a car and tell what was wrong with it. Even some of the managers from the mine brought their fancy cars to us. I was their go-fer. Uncle Richard wanted his own car, but the grocery didn't pay much.

I heard Mommy say one time, out of Richard's hearing, that he'd never be able to afford a family without working in the mines. I know that bothered Daddy and started him scheming. That was another thing Daddy was good at. If he wanted something, he generally figured a way to get it.

One Saturday Daddy borrowed Uncle Hershel's truck, and he and Uncle Richard were gone all day. When they came back that night, they trailered the ugliest car I ever saw. It was a dark colored Dodge that had a lot of rust on it and I could hardly wait for them to get out the Bondo and the paint and make it pretty. They could do magic making an ugly car look like what Daddy called "snazzy." I wanted them to paint it baby blue. Maybe even put flames on the sides of the hood, but they never even bothered with the body. They cleaned it up a little, but mostly they worked on the engine, and as they worked, I could hear the speed in that car, just like they did.

One night I guessed they were about done with the engine and I asked, "Is that a courtin' car?" Daddy laughed. Said it was a car to make little girls ask questions.

"Will you take me a ride?" I asked.

Uncle Richard looked at Daddy and his eyes got crinkly, and I ran and jumped in the back seat before they had a chance to think about it and say no.

It was a hot night and the cool air felt good. Uncle Richard drove slow with Daddy in the suicide seat and we got out of the hollow and on down to the highway to Beckwith. Daddy waited until there was no traffic, turned and looked at Richard and said, "Open her up."

Uncle Richard turned back toward me and told me to sit behind Daddy and hold on tight. I did, and I've never been so fast in a car as I was that night. I didn't need to hold on because I was pushed back in the seat like the hand of God was on my chest. I could hardly breathe. That Dodge made two sounds when Uncle Richard shifted gears and I could feel a tug as if the car was making up its mind how fast it would go. It was like we were flying all the way to Beckwith; then at the city limits, we slowed down like a snail. We went to the ice cream store and Daddy got us all a cone of ice cream, and before he gave me mine, he said "If you ever tell your Mommy anything about this car, I will not let you hang around with us anymore, as God is my witness, Lindy." I took an imaginary key, locked my mouth and threw the key out the window. Daddy said, "All right, then." That was the best ice cream I ever had in my life.

A few nights after that, Uncle Richard, Uncle Hershel

and I went down to the old barn. They took out the back seat and put in a metal box that went from the backseat into the trunk. It was getting just good and dark and Daddy and Richard said they had to take the car out to test it. Daddy asked Hershel did he want a ride home and Hershel said there wasn't no room and he'd just walk with me, so Daddy and Richard took off and when me and Uncle Hershel were nearly home, Uncle Hershel kissed me and stuck his tongue in my mouth and put his hand on my pants. I pulled back my fist and hit him as hard as I could right in the eye. Hershel grabbed his face and swore. I said, "If you ever touch me again, I'll tell Daddy." He said he never would, and he left me to find my own way home, which I could've done blind from anywhere in Mud Hollow.

  I was sleeping sound when I was woken up by Daddy and Mommy having words. Mommy said all us kids needed shoes and Daddy spent shoe money to help Uncle Richard buy his car. Daddy said if he had to, he knew how to cut the toes out of shoes to make them last as long as they needed to. He said he had been a planner all his life and he could take care of his own family and not one of us'd ever gone hungry and she'd soon see that he knew what he was doing.

  After that, every few nights, Uncle Richard would stay out all night and come home in the morning. Mommy said not to play around the house and to keep our voices down so Uncle Richard could get some sleep before he went in to the IGA. He and Daddy still worked on cars, but not as much. I asked Mommy where Uncle Richard had got to and she said he was most likely courting, though she couldn't see it because he couldn't afford to get married. Then she laughed and said she reckoned she and Daddy couldn't afford to either.

  It wasn't long before Uncle Richard brought home some

pork and Mommy fixed it with beans. It took me about an hour to eat because I wanted to taste every bite, it was so good. And before us kids started school, Mommy took us to the store and bought us each a brand-new pair of shoes, and not from the Goodwill either. We were the first ones to wear them.

Uncle Richard also brought home a canning jar. He and Daddy went out on the porch and drank the water out of it. Daddy snorted and Uncle Richard giggled. Mommy was in a bad mood the next day.

When Mommy had her birthday in May, Uncle Richard and Daddy went into town and brought her back a radio with a record player and records. Mommy was so surprised she cried. Mommy kept the radio on all day and all night. We heard Wolfman Jack, Juicey Brucie in Boston, and Dick Biondi in Chicago. I couldn't get enough.

Mommy and I were listening to the records the night the police knocked on the door. Daddy and Uncle Richard went outside to talk to them and only Daddy came back in. They took Uncle Richard to jail for bootlegging. The judge gave Uncle Richard a choice: jail or the army, and he chose the army. Before we knew it, he was in Vietnam.

After that, we listened to the news instead of music, while Daddy wrung his hands, paced, and prayed. Then came the telegram that Uncle Richard was missing in action.

That night Daddy got out a Mason jar and sat on the porch drinking. Late in the night I heard him stumbling down the porch. I fell asleep and was awakened by Daddy's whistle. It echoed through Mud Hollow from one end to the other all night long. In the morning, neighbors brought

Daddy home and Mommy put him to bed.

Army officers came later in the week to tell us they'd found Uncle Richard and he was coming back home, but not the way we wanted. The folks in Mud Hollow said the only reason they found Uncle Richard was because Daddy whistled him home.

Everyone in the Hollow came to Uncle Richard's funeral. His casket was covered with a flag and at the end of the service, men in uniform shot their guns into the air. Daddy jumped at the gunshots like a bad hound. Soldiers folded Uncle Richard's flag and gave it to Daddy. It terrified me to see Daddy sob; he couldn't stop. But when it was time, he got up and put the first handful of dirt onto the casket. Uncle Hershel and Uncle Gray held him up.

I never saw Daddy take a drink after that day. Uncle Richard was given a medal for bravery and it hung on our living room wall. As long as he lived, every July 16, Daddy would wait till sundown and then walk to Uncle Richard's grave, whistling and waiting for Richard's answering whistle. Whistling and waiting.

We buried Daddy and Mommy next to Uncle Richard.

Every year on Decoration Day, I put a flag at Uncle Richard's grave and flowers on all three of their graves. I never could whistle like Daddy did, but I learned how to make a circle with my thumb and third finger and whistle. Before I leave their graves, I always whistle just to let each of them know where I am, and that I miss them and I'm on my way home.

Sherry Poff

In Secret Places

From the shade of a maple on my lawn,
a swift form emerges, disappears
in darkness farther on.
Another glimpse of wings on grass
pulls my gaze upward just in time
to see him pass.
He walks the wind in perfect silence,
wrapped in light, at last discovered
by the shadow of his presence.

Patsy Kisner
Black Walnut

Summer sun
glints across your surface,
particularly the core
of your heart
that blooms across
the coffee table.

The bookcase gleams
of arching, deepening
grain—
light reflecting
with such shining
that I watch
to see if there is
a side to the prism
that will shift back
the brightest green
of leaves.

Patricia Hope

The Secret Is...

Your first letter to me was written
on an envelope opened up
because you didn't have any paper.

In its words secrets to read again and again—
the cost of items you bought in 1962—$2.00
for a hat, $1.20 for gloves—so you could work
in a frigid Chicago February on the freight docks
to earn money to send for me and to rent us an apartment.

The money you wired for bus fare picked up
at Western Union with only the answer to one question –
what is your favorite candy bar? Your welcome home
when I arrived, our tiny refrigerator holding
a single box of Hershey Bars.

John C. Mannone

The Making of Steel

Crush ore into inch-round pieces:
magnetite, hematite, goethite, limonite,
or ferrous carbonate called siderite.
Geochemistry can sound so poetic.

Water-shower and wash away all
the clay, dirt, loam through weir and sieve.

Throw ore through throats of earthen furnaces
with charcoal fire inside. Roast it. Drive water
from the washings, and water tied-up in crystal
mineral. Expel impurities like sulfur.

Bellow air—increase heat. Let carbon ooze
from fuel into the molten mass smelted in
the mouths of furnaces. Upwind, watch them
breathe out gases from incomplete combustion.

Collect porous metal mixed with slag—
the bloom to be forged into wrought iron.
Heat, fold, beat, quench repeatedly. Then

injure beyond insult: tread on her air
with carbon footprints, then fashion
wrought iron into steel shovels
to spade earth, strip her of her coal,
feed her overburdened heart to river fish.

Before the invention of the blast furnace (1828), Kentucky built the first charcoal iron furnace (1791) to make wrought iron, precursor of steel.

Richard Hague

What I Had Instead of Stories

That dark jubilating Isaiah of mill and smoke marrow.
—James Wright, on my hometown

The ones I tell and have told for years
I made up. Mostly, there were no stories:
noisy town, railroads, steel mills—
cacophonies and cinders.
Old men and women hardly had voices.
The hills no longer spoke tongues.
I couldn't hear myself breathe,
and so any love I might have learned,
any grief I might have had to swallow,
any hope I might have had to dream up:
throw it out and turn away, boy, turn away.

And why wouldn't I, the air so bad
it was famous? Safer to suck in and hold
what I had to tell for later, when I could
hide in my future and testify
on paper, out of their sight and hearing.

I never wanted to say bad about my town,
except when I did. Even then, no regrets.
Everything, even the bad, I knew,
would go up in smoke.

Carson Colenbaugh

Copperhill

> Ducktown, TN
> After Lamar Dodd's painting *Copperhill,* c. 1938

I.

Onto the dirt road with my friend behind the wheel,
    trespassing deep inside
The private Company bounds of the Copper Basin just to
    see the hills. The ore companies
Came when they couldn't find gold, denuded each red hill
    for some chance at a dollar,
Came up lucky. Virginia pines alone germinate in
    shadows of soil, pulling toxins,
Remediating sin as a preacher pulls demons from raging
    blood. The sky emerging
In the image of a storm fogs the rusty hillside, ravages
    gullies that still show
Like marks on this tired body. Ducktown residents sued
    the Company in 1907
For their damages. Smelters poisoned land, rended the
    guts of livestock. The case went
To the high court, who shut up the Company to history.
    Still, more came around
Drilling, blasting pennies from the deep, burning earth
    into storms of sulfur and soot.

II.

Last winter in the art museum, brush strokes soaked that
    desolation in palettes
Of charcoal, burnt brick, sandstone, an emptiest black. I
    wrapped you in my arms,
Settled my chin in the valley of your neck and pointed to
    the painting, its color,
Each hidden carcass. I told you how men churned the
    sunken copper hills
Into acid pits, how oxides were dug straight like this
    memory writ plainly
On tight canvas in egg tempera. I told you about the
    foreman shack, about Lamar Dodd's
High-rolled sleeves and the cruelty of our commerce,
    about my vision of place.
On the far side of the hill unseen, perhaps a home for the
    two of us. Everything we own
Hanging out on a droopy cotton line. Goats, sheep, hens,
    warm skin, grass,
Fat blossoms of coneflowers come spring. May we plant
    something more equal to love
Than another cold ore drill. May we roll up our own
    sleeves and get to work.

William Scott Hanna
Homecoming

In this new after-death
I've come back
to the only house on the left,

not knowing if
I will ever come back to life
at all,
but here,
at least—

wind in the locust trees,
the shadow of youth,
the memory of this place

being everything,
scent of pine and sound of birdsong,
the smell of apples

just before the fall.

Michael Templeton
Strata and Flows

The Appalachian Counties in southeastern Ohio have some magnificent hiking trails. They are not heavily traveled, and this is what I like most about them. I can walk these trails and forget all about everything, including myself. Driving out to the trail, you can see the way the 21st century is layering itself over the 20th century. There are vast farms, huge corn and soybean operations. There are cattle, a few sheep and goats, and even an alpaca herd up on a northern hillside. The road is dotted with big service stations that offer lottery tickets, energy drinks, pizza, and roller food. The remnants of old family-owned diners are filled with eyebrow shops and tattoo shops. Of course, fast food is ubiquitous. Trump signs in yards, "Let's Go Brandon" signs, and the odd confederate flag tell you a little about the area. Beneath all of this, there are the artifacts of other centuries, and to see these artifacts, you need to travel on foot.

The trailhead is marked by a large wooden sign that explains the rules. No dogs, no motorized vehicles (local folks will still ride their ATVs when they can get away with it), no alcohol, and no littering. You are also told to stay on the trail. Wandering off the trail can damage the natural systems, and it can lead you into someone else's property. Bearing right, I head slightly uphill through some thick pines. Toward the top of the hill, I spot a dirt mound about six feet in diameter and at least four feet high. These hills are made by Allegheny mound ants. These are a large species of ant, and they can be quite aggressive.

The ants would be invisible amid the brush and undergrowth if not for the enormous mounds where the ants do something remarkable. These ants are ranchers. Allegheny mound ants love the honeydew produced by aphids and the larva of other small insects. Since the ants feast on the honeydew, they tend the aphids and larvae like livestock. Beneath the industrial farms and the herds of cattle, these ants tend to their own herds and flocks. A favorite of the Allegheny mound ant is the Edwards Hairstreak butterfly. The ants tend to the butterfly pupae in the mounds, and they carry them into the surrounding trees so it can feed. The pupae then release the honeydew that feeds the ants. This relationship has become a feature of the lifecycle of both species. The ants feed and thrive on the honeydew. The Edwards Hairstreak butterfly completes its lifecycle with the assistance of the Allegheny mound ants. It all takes place silently and invisibly under the brush and foliage of the meadow and the surrounding woods.

At the top end of a slight hillside, I can see a farm to the left, a mix of meadow and trees to the right. In the summer months, this section of the trail is so dense with growth you cannot see beyond a few feet into the trees. The winter trail is more barren, and I can see where the preservation organization has mowed large swathes of the meadow and cut back young trees. Decades of farming have changed the soil conditions so profoundly that the land cannot support the natural progression of foliage and trees. While hardwoods will take root and grow, they will die once they reach a certain stage in maturity because the soil cannot support them. The meadow requires careful management with a strategic balance of grasses, brush, and conifers before it can support the growth that made up the forests that thrived here before early American colonizers domesticated the land. This kind of strategic management allows us to see the layers and strata of the centuries.

Gilles Deleuze and Felix Guattari provide a theory of human culture and the natural world that talks about strata and flows in a mind-boggling book called *A Thousand Plateaus:*

Capitalism and Schizophrenia. You can safely live your life without ever reading it, but if you choose to suffer through it, it does provide some useful insights. They explain that natural systems unfold over centuries and millennia and tend to form strata. Natural systems form layers so that one stratum becomes the foundation for the next. Culture tends to operate in flows. A cultural system—a specific type of agriculture for example—begins to take hold, and it flows outward across the land. Humans are good at adapting flows to different conditions, but the flows interrupt and exploit the natural strata. For most of human history, the strata seemed inexhaustible. The Earth was endless, and culture could flow without end along the strata of the Earth. But here's the hitch: cultural flows begin to calcify and form strata, and the natural strata bear the weight of the human presence. As a result, the natural strata get used up, exposed, and refuse to support the cultural systems that have now formed heavy and dense human strata. You can see the strata of the Earth and the calcified strata of culture as you drive the rural state route out to the trail. You can also see it in the meadow and woods as the ground itself refuses to yield the foliage it once supported effortlessly, secretly, and silently.

As I said, it is winter. I can see into the wooded areas that surround the meadow. I spot a house in the woods, and I decide to break some rules. I cut through the dead brush up to the house and find that it is completely abandoned. The gravel driveway that once connected the house and the lot to the road is overgrown. There are three outbuildings in varying stages of ruin and decay, and one is nearly filled with old paint cans. I've already broken the rules by veering off the trail, so I decide to go ahead and break the law by checking out the abandoned house.

The old house is typical of the type of farmhouses that

characterize this part of the country. White wooden siding still clings to the exterior. The windows still have glass in them, although a few of them are broken. Inside there is litter all over the floors in almost every room. Most striking is the presence of clothing scattered throughout the house as if the last occupant had to leave in a hurry. There are shoes still laid out in pairs on the floor. On the second floor, clothing still hangs on hangers from nails in the wall. The floors are also strewn with old newspapers, magazines, and mail. An old Sear's catalogue from 1977, a newspaper from 1956, and an old issue of *Reader's Digest*. The layers and strata of human history are spread out on the floors, and the layers and strata of someone's life are everywhere visible. It was all left behind for reasons I cannot know or even guess. The lives that once inhabited this house are strata that gave way to newer flows that move at the speed of light.

    I discovered a small section of wall space that obviously had been behind a woodstove. The opening for the stovepipe was visible. Beneath the peeling wallpaper I could see the artifacts of years, of people's lives in that house. Patched into and onto the wall there was a fragment of a Gold Medal Flour bag, the circle with the word "Medal" clearly visible. I saw tin can lids and corrugated cardboard from packing boxes. The ancient tar paper was visible in some spots. There were layers of wallpaper. A fragment of the paper still retained the design of what looked like hand painted ivy and berries climbing up the wall against an off-white background; an image of brush and foliage that once surrounded the house remains, and its delicate images still shine through the decay.

    Looking at this spot of wall I could see the layers and strata of the rural life that once flowed, before it was stratified and buried under other strata, before the tattoo shops, sprawling service stations, the fast-food joints, before the land had to be healed by strategic management. I could see what remained of a time when the human flows still thrived off the natural strata, and the illusory promise of an endless and limitless Earth, flows as quiet and anonymous as the Edwards Hairstreak butterfly and the Allegheny mound builder ants. This was life that came and passed with nothing to reveal but the corn, soybeans, and milk that fed the nation.

Strata and flows are neither right nor wrong. They are indifferent. And there is no reason to assume that human flows are more important than any other. We now face the real possibility that all human flows will simply cease. The strata of the past centuries suggest that we not become overly proud of the flows of the present. These too will calcify and turn to strata. The strata will make way for different flows that will not include us. It is not even a matter of turning to dust and bones. It will be as if we never lived at all.

Tommye Scanlin

Five Leaves For Miss Lillian

Woven tapestry using hand-dyed wool and natural materials (indigo, madder, cochineal, black walnut, weld)

Carol Parris Krauss

The Old Folks Warn You About the Willow Tree

The old folks say a willow should never be planted close to a home's water system or pipes. The roots will seek out and wrap the plumbing and drain field. In a quest to fill their endless thirst, the rhiza can render an entire sewer system useless.

You almost missed the c-section. Squeamish. Not sure you could stand the cutting. Skin and muscle unzipping. Clamped. In the end, you stayed. Gathered hands in a circle with nurses and the doctor for pre-surgery prayer. Happy to be the first to hold, hoist the baby.

All smiles. Early on you traveled annually to the foothills. To sit with my family, watch us shuck Silver Queen on the bottom porch, pull stories from our Blue Ridge ancestors.

Soaking up tales of how the French Broad flooded when Mother was five, laughing when Uncle Bill showed us how to use a divining rod under the shadow of Mount Pisgah. For seven years, you drank in all you could hold. Then some.

Photos from that last year show you at the edge of each photo frame, holiday table, and reunion. Or behind the camera, on the couch sleeping. Hand strewn over your face. With time, you faded from the pictures. No longer sitting by the fireplace, immersed in the stories of Uncle Gilbert

or the last family trip to Myrtle beach. Now elsewhere. Underground. Busy creeping to new waters. Crawling to a new home to grab and strangle it with gnarled, dirty hands. Wring it dry.

Taylor Roberts

For the Record

you have to stay up late
to get him to talk about it
maybe a little drunk, and then
you're lucky to hear
any scrap from the past
crush and collect it like the pop cans
you helped him recycle
when they were worth something—
the older the memory, the better
ten-year-old Grandpa pulling a knife
on the school bus bully
the road was dirt and the field full of cattle
that needed tending to
more than schoolwork, anyhow
later, he looked forward to going to work
in the Austinville mines until
he got laid off and she did too
they needed food stamps
for one month—just one
no great family secrets
he just can't hardly fathom why
you'd want to hear about it

Dale Farmer

Never Out of My Heart

A man never knows who he is until he knows where he's come from.
—Charlie Abner, *The Mountain Minor*

    Why do so many people hate the banjo? What is it about the timbre of vibrating steel strings amplified by a plastic head stretched over a wood rim that evokes mockery and condescension? I only have a minor in psychology so I'm not an expert on such but during banjo performances when onlookers start with that all too familiar, silly, exaggerated hillbilly dance and yell out "Deliverance," it feels like more than just a stringed instrument being denigrated.

    My parents were the first generation in my family not born in Eastern Kentucky. Dad had a good-paying job that supported our family's suburban lifestyle. We were a "normal" family living in a nice neighborhood in Fairfield, just north of Cincinnati. We had a white framed house, a trimmed lawn and a brand new 1970 blue Pontiac Catalina in the driveway. We kids played sports, got good grades and other than wearing clothes from the on-sale rack at Kmart and the occasional soup beans and cornbread for supper, nothing about our lifestyle bore residue of Appalachia. We were middle class Ohioans and all was well with the world. All was well until something went terribly wrong—I began playing the banjo.

    I was a kid most often found building forts in the woods behind our house or catching minnows, tadpoles and crawdads in the nearby Pleasant Run Creek. My maternal grandparents, Charley and Ida Cox, lived on a farm a few miles away near West Chester raising cattle, horses and a very large garden that kept them in canned goods year-round. There were acres and acres of woods with trails and a creek that called to me constantly. My dad and I would sometimes saddle up horses and take a bag of tin cans and a couple of guns with us down the trail and into the woods. We'd line the cans up on a downed tree and pretend that they were Jesse James, Billy the Kid and Johnny Ringo drawing down on us as our bullets sent them outlaw cans a flying.

  I often watched Grandma skin rabbits and squirrels, clean freshly caught fish and break green beans. She ran me out of the house whenever she canned, declaring the pressure cooker would explode and be the demise of us all. She cooked three hot meals every day and there was nearly always a combination of aunts, uncles, cousins, friends and neighbors there to help eat it all. Grandpa had worked his way up from illiterate migrant to Public Works Director for the Village of Evendale. Grandma often cooked a hot midday meal for Grandpa's entire road crew. Because it was cooked, my grandparents called it dinner. They always took great pleasure in feeding anyone who ever entered their home and feeding them more than they could comfortably eat. They always encouraged additional helpings, if Grandma herself wasn't already plopping another big spoonful or a chicken leg onto their plates. I imagine their generosity sprang from once not knowing if there would be enough to feed the family to their newfound bounty in the land of plenty.

  I loved spending all the time my parents would allow living that Appalachian lifestyle on the farm with my grandparents. Even as a young boy I sensed a constant voice echoing through those Kentucky Mountains and calling Grandpa back home. I couldn't get enough of his stories of growing up in Jackson County, Kentucky as I imagined living them out myself. I never realized their Kentucky life was much romanticized in my young mind. I couldn't feel the pangs of hunger as I imagined playing in the mountains. I couldn't feel the anxiety and uncertainty for the lack of medical care for my children, or wonder if the gardens would produce enough to feed us through the winter. I never imagined the worry on my father's face when he couldn't find work to supplement his off-the-grid sustenance.

The first time my grandparents took me to Kentucky I experienced a strangely familiar feeling; seeing mountains for the first time along the Mountain Parkway. I wanted Grandpa to stop the car and let me run to them. We stayed in the old log farmhouse with no electricity or plumbing and had to draw the sweetest water from the well out front. Grandma cooked our meals on the wood-fired cookstove. I got to run and play in the mountains. I experienced a brief taste of the romanticized life Grandpa told of that I had longed for. I so wished I were Appalachian.

Many of Grandpa's accounts were of playing music at night when the work was done and fiddling for square dances and singing the old hymns at the Pentecostal church. These were the stories I loved most. All four of my grandparents were musicians and I wanted to be just like them in any way I could. Grandpa loaned me his old banjo with the promise of giving it to me if I learned to play it. Mom tells me I was always somewhat of a loner. When there were other kids around, I would be happily playing by myself. At family reunions when all the cousins were off playing together, I sat in the circle with the old men listening to them complain about politicians and the price of bacon and tell stories of the old days back in Kentucky. Other teenagers I knew were more successful at hiding their Appalachian heritage. They cruised the hometown streets with radios blaring Journey, Aerosmith and the Doobie Brothers while I was at home in my bedroom playing along with my Earl Scruggs, Bill Monroe and Stanley Brothers records.

Grandpa's old banjo was a priceless gift. I could play it and feel connected with family long gone as the notes of my heritage vibrated throughout my body and soul. I once played a special banjo instrumental at my church. I poured every ounce of my being into "In the Sweet Bye and Bye." I received a few compliments, but it was received as nothing more than a novelty by most. A few church members actually complained of having to endure hearing a twangy banjo in the house of God. "Praise the Lord with the stringed instruments, unless it's a banjo" (Psalms 150:4). The minister's wife told a group of church ladies "Dale is so talented but it's just too bad he doesn't play real music." My own wife hated the banjo. So, to preserve the marriage and not risk eternal damnation I gave up playing it. For the 25 years the marriage lasted I was the dutiful suburban husband with the nice house, a manicured lawn and a banjo with rusty strings tucked away under the bed.

I've learned that Appalachian identity is a common and often conflicting theme for those of us a generation or two removed from the great migration. My grandparents were from Kentucky, but I'd never considered my own identity having anything to do with Appalachia. Geographically, I was an Ohioan and until recent years a more internal heritage identity was a notion I'd never considered. For so long the music was out of my hands but never out of my heart. That voice Grandpa heard echoing through the mountains still calls and now I'm compelled to answer.

I load up my banjo in the Jeep and head southward. As the Mountain Parkway horizon comes into view, that wonderfully familiar feeling returns as I reminisce traveling there with my grandparents many years before. I again ponder Grandpa's words, "A man never knows who he is until he knows where he's come from," but now with a sense of belonging. I often go out of my way to visit old family cemeteries and always wish I could find an old dirt road that would take me back to 1932. I'm grateful to be one of the lucky ones that can play the same notes and tunes that my grandparents first heard and played nearly a hundred years ago; that I can carry on the family musical traditions and preserve the memories of my heritage; that I can sit on an old porch in Jackson County, Kentucky with my banjo and somehow feel my grandparents sitting next to me playing along. This has been a most rewarding journey of self-discovery, of realizing what has always been there, what I've always been: Appalachian.

McKenna Revel
My Mother's Father's First Story

He could remember when all they had was a house. No running water, no electricity, no heat, no air, just a house. They used kerosene lamps for light; I've seen one of them. Pretty, antique thing with a porcelain base and pastel flowers on the front. A frivolous relic. Someone's only source of brightness in darkness. Before the first lightbulb. He could remember the first lightbulb. Naked. No porcelain cover. *But boy*, he said, *it lit up*! Lit up like his facial expression sixty years later, lit up like his voice, lit up like the ends of the cigarettes that killed him. He went on, *I said, look! You can see all the way under the table! If we had the same light now, we would call it darkness.* But he never forgot that light. Not even when he began to forget the way home. I never forgot the story. Not even when I was thankful to the cigarettes for taking him first. His face in my mind's eye every time I flick a switch.

Todd Davis

Where Fisher Go to Die

Six Septembers ago I stumbled upon you,
face shoveling the abdomen of a porcupine,
ravenous pleasure paused, shoulders hunched
to see if I posed a threat, jaws wet
and red, eyes that said joy was in eating the eyes
of another. Three winters after that afternoon,
while I hunted a deer whose heart I hoped to eat,
I found the place you went to die. A gray day.
Rain turning to snow. Interior of the mountain
where it comes together in two folds. Rock lip
that led to a narrowing cave. I only wanted in
from the weather. Expected porcupine turds,
hickory nuts forgotten by chipmunks and squirrels.
Instead the skeletons of all the fisher who'd lived
in this place. Who'd avoided our traps, our guns.
Who'd come with age and weariness, stomachs
starting to empty, to lay down in the half-light
of this rock, to return, after so much isolation,
to their kin. The bones took the form of a door.
Eye sockets looking back toward the cave's
entrance. Maybe imagining that early pink light
in March when their mothers drew them
from between legs, slick with the blood
they'd soon crave.

Gabriel Dunsmith

The Raveling

To take up the not-life,
    to bury it in sedge,
        to watch dusk bronze the leaves which were once golden,

to trip over an old shoe,
    to let the husk fall from your arm, and keep on falling,
        to lie amongst the dew-draped sorrel,

to wade softly through the canebrake as snapping turtles lie in wait,
    to praise the eager needle of the heron's beak,
        to point the antler due north,

to stumble into an otter's den,
    to hang moth wings on a telephone wire,
        to recount your gilded dream to the recluse,

to turn round in deep woods, unsure of the way you came,
    to drop a pearl of sand down the blacksnake's throat,
        to snare a will-o'-wisp,

to skim stones across the lake of your desire,
    to clasp a locket over a single thorn,
        to open it to find a feather,

to note the declensions in your neighbor's cry,
    to cup your ear to the well's rim,
        to feel the tremble of a teacup calls you home.

Jackie Ison Kalbli
If My Best Face Forward Came Off,

underneath would be thick migrant skin
grooved like a scratchy 78 RPM
Jimmy Rodger's rendition of "California Blues"
where they sleep out every night…

You would see my forehead is scorched
like women in *The Grapes of Wrath* movie,
when their California dreams hardened
into another bowl of dust.

I wasn't on this earth
for the shortage of wrinkle cream,
but Mom told me
about when the WPA
camped out all the able-bodies
from the hollers back home in Elliott County,
and families ate again,
and depression was gone,
and then the war came,
and things were even better,
because of Oak Ridge and
the Manhattan Project.

Dad and Mom left everything
everybody every notion
of how to be in the world
to move north to Ohio
where jobs were grapes on the vine
but blight spoiled the crop

and passed to me a hunger
biting behind polished teeth
that makes stubbed-toe poor
in the tobacco barn
seem like Beverly Hills.

Jim Minick
The Collar

More than its beak that daggers the suet,
more than its whispers or squawks or pointed
crown, more even than the soft back
that looks like fur, not feathers,
gray fading to blue down the spine,
more than anything else, the blue jay
is defined by its collar, so black—
a lawyer's without the tie,
a queen's tight monarchy of the sky,
a priest's without the sanctity,
where a nest found is a nest eaten.

Or the collar could be this: a noose
that knots at the top of the head, burn
marks from a rope, a mythological
scar for some unknown crime, history
worn as jewelry, a stunning reminder
of our own mad and ugly past.

PAULETTA HANSEL

Presidents Day 2021

I.
Friend, I can't stop thinking about race,
today, and by race, I mean whiteness,
mine and yours, and if I am honest (I am trying
to be honest), that of almost everyone
I know. This neighborhood is getting whiter,
and I'm not talking about the February snow
that coats our cars and lawns and sidewalks.
Fifteen years ago, we were the nice white couple
next door, across the street, backyard abutting yard.
Now there's too many of us for me to count.
Our Black Lives Matter signs are staked in lawns
where black children played.
My husband's children
called these tree-lined cul-de-sacs
the ghetto.
I'd like to say we moved here, then,
to give his suburban teens a better view.
In truth, we moved here for those trees,
this house, the yard,
the picture of the kind of whiteness
we might learn to be.
But mixed neighborhoods
don't mean we don't still sort ourselves by color,
like to like.

II.
Today I walk the snow-packed streets, composing
in my mind these lines.

I am careful where I put my foot. This whiteness
covers ice and cracks I cannot see.
The scarf that's wrapped around my neck—
gold-flecked black against the cardinal red
of my down coat—was given to me
by black women I love. Their hands
eased my mother's pain; their faces
ease my memory of her years of dying.
We hold her close by keeping each other near.
And still, we are so careful.
We watch where we step.

III.
Friend, do you remember where you were 2008,
Election Day, Barack Obama?
Of course, you do.
In this room where I now write, I watched
his victory speech recorded on the internet,
Michelle dressed in red on black, starlight beside him.
I cheered my silent cheers while my stepdaughter slept.
I'd taken her to see some fluff of white girls
whining on the movie screen.
I tried to fill and smooth the cracks
between us, then.
Now she bemoans all the ways her family
raised her to be racist.
As we did.
As we all were raised,
we who are white.

IV.
I know I told you of my father's march for justice,
Main Street, Richmond, Kentucky, May 1961.

White stones thrown against our house.
I probably never shared the story my parents told me,
how at five-years-old I'd tried to talk away their tears
during Walter Cronkite, 1965, the bloody march
from Selma to Montgomery:
"It's okay," I told them,
"They're only black."
from Selma to Montgomery:
"It's okay," I told them,
"They're only black."

V.
I wear my whiteness lightly,
like a down-filled coat. I hardly know
it's there, unless I'm called out to the cold
without it. And, friend, how often am I
called to that?

Scott T. Hutchison

Equality

You have blood-brother hallowed rules
for the flour bombing of houses:
you cannot know *who*, you cannot care *who*.
Randomness makes everybody equal.

You've learned, firsthand, how the *evenhanded* treatment
of offenders in your high school isn't uniform, isn't impartial:
if you're pretty, or well-bred, if you say *yes sir* and *no ma'am*
with respectful tone—if your clothes are labeled and clean,
no traces of smoke or mildew—then you receive a nod and
a *warning*. Maybe more than what most classmates consider
a fair share. And all the while pounded with educational gospels,
smiley-face pronouncements of us all building with perfectly
level opportunities in a new and better tomorrow.

Same old world. An epic story of smiles, winks, *words*.
Lectures with little practical reality. But you and your buddy
who's earned the name Cheeseburger by devouring the entire thing
in one bite, the eat-it deal being you buy for him every time
since he never has money—you and Cheese actually listened
in history class, then looked to the old world's artillery;
you two dullards built yourselves a siege-engine trebuchet
in shop class using ancient engineering, strong wood
paid for with tax dollars. Positive results from that teaching moment:
and so you glide through holy star-filled nights, selecting ridgelines
with unsystematic care, seek out shadowed corners, covered
beneath hemlock night-shade. You've learned how to guesstimate
sixty yards. A culmination of patient study and skills: completing
road trips to grocery stores two hours away in any direction,

stocking up with bags of Gold Medal.
Content and slumbery people settled down from a day's worries—
jumping at the sudden thumping from above, thinking God
or the Devil's footprint has angrily stamped on the rooftop.
in Their name you rain five pounds of sifted revelation
on the anys and the everys, dust up the eaves with puffy bursts
of paper, a fine thud of heavenly cloud. It's always silly
and beautiful. The whole-house community rushing out,
panicked in the same flabbergasted way. While the truth

floats breezily down upon them. You grab and run. On a mission
to find another mansion or shack, trailer, duplex, a quaint
landscaped cottage. You sling a small weight high, watch
the parabolic lesson descend. A storm will wash it all away—
everything powdered will dissolve to fine. You and Cheeseburger

wink. Nothing to say. Some people learn that craziness
arbitrarily rains out of the sky—that God forgets
your name, your cleverness, your sins
and your smirk of safety—God, who knows
how much mysterious and prophetic instruction
you've failed to regard—God, who will
drop a bag of flour on your head,
maybe worse. Maybe the answer
is someone worse. Everybody should know this.

Gerald Smith

Omen

Beyond the weathering house, behind the paired maples
Older than this house so second on this farm,
All now gone to weed: briar, honeysuckle, creeper;
Saplings showered by seed from a line of poplars.
The road leads past the barn musty with last crop of hay
Moldering twenty years past, burrow of mice and worms,
Pantry to shiny black snakes coiled between rotting studs.
Beyond the barn a garden,
Wire fence absorbed into trees now living posts
Marking edge bounding long folds of furrows,
Giving up harvest of sedge, tangle of blackberry, invasive cedar,
All emissaries of the distant wood lot
Redeeming piecemeal this cleared land, restoring it,
Healing it of the ancient wounds of plow and hoe,
A garden ungrowing itself into forest free of dream or need.
Standing under a dark tree, tight circle of afternoon shade
I reached into the branches and pulled down an apple,
Old variety, heirloom, hard, black green not store bin red,
To show my gathered students so they might unkey this spot,
Reverse the work of succession and imagine life of house,
Children, livestock, labor on land now invisible to care.
Her eyes grew wide. I saw her lips move as if ready
For sacrament in wildwood church
When I sliced the apple and offered her a piece,
Wet with sap on the blade of my knife.
Taste brought recognition more than dark mottled skin
As she blurted, "An apple," then confessed,
Forgetting ancient curse of first garden
That led by trail of tears and sorrow

To this garden of labor and sweat,
"I have never eaten anything from a tree before."
Leaving me to wonder if new knowledge
Had returned her in child-like awe to innocence
Or if snakes had been omen
And I had destroyed Eden yet again.

Elaine Fowler Palencia
Fleeing Eden

A long trip for short legs
we made through town and
into the soft arms of the country
my father in overalls
pushing the wheelbarrow
I dancing beside him
in high summer
down a dirt road
past an old woman sitting
on an older porch
into deep trees
beside a dark lake
and around the lake
to the head of a hollow
where in a clearing
the ground still bore
the outline of a homestead
and a gnarled apple tree
stood by limestone steps
that ended in air.
Under the tree
lay a headless doll
with a hole for a navel.
We ate red apples
heady as hard cider
and my father set a sieve over the barrow
shoveled on hen house soil
shook the sieve to make fine dirt
for our vegetable garden

until with a shout
eyes rolling like a horse gone loco
he pulled me away from where
the loam seethed with snakes
wriggling from dead pearls.
Hindbrains in recoil
we hastened away, but not before
I realized my father was mortal.
Thus I fell into dualism,
as one does in Eden.

Chrissie Anderson Peters
Marking

Let me proffer a proper warning:
I believe in making my mark.
I believe in leaving some part of me—
Living, not living—behind for
Sometime when someone,
Somewhere, for whatever reason
Needs something.
Something bigger, something fuller,
Something deeper than it feels like
Can survive in mere existence.

I believe in making a name
For things without words,
Places that are lost on maps
Full of place names
And street addresses,
Places of the heart and mind
In time-space, future-past.
Naming the nameless,
Blazing blank slates—
Mark my words.

MIKE SCHOEFFEL

My Buddy Evan

My buddy Evan, he says things I don't agree with. One time he was driving us to The Watering Hole in his Honda Accord so we could have a couple Tuesday night beers when we got caught between lights. It was wet out and Evan slammed on the brakes. The driver in the Camry behind us was following too close so she ran into us pretty hard. Enough to bend her hood back pretty good.

At first we thought, dang, she must be hurt, bad collision and all. Evan, on the whole, is a solid guy, so am I, at least that's what I like to believe, so we walk back to check on the driver. When she rolls down the window the first thing I notice is she's black, and I think *here we go*, because I know Evan's history with that sort of thing. The second thing I notice is there's a baby, maybe a year old, in the passenger seat, not in a car seat, nothing. Evan and I, we're shocked. I think: *Well that ain't right*, but say nothing, because nobody was injured, and I figure the police will take care of it, write her a ticket, or hand down some other fitting punishment. Evan, though, I can feel him boiling. Tenser than hell. But he doesn't say anything, because like I mentioned, he's a pretty nice guy when the water hits the well. I've known him for a long time and this is what I've noticed.

So eventually the fire department shows up and moves our cars to the side of the road and now the four of us are just hanging around, waiting on the police. It's drizzling, and the red lights on the fire truck are going round and round but the siren is off. Evan and I are leaning up against his Accord, cursing, muttering. He packs a dip into the corner of his mouth. The woman is seated on her trunk with the baby next to her. The baby is straight up and watching cars fly past with these big eyes full of curiosity and confusion, like he's thinking *what am I doing here and what on Earth are these things whizzing past me?* Evan and I, we look at the baby, start to calm down.

Evan checks his phone, says "Damn, looks like we're going to miss happy hour." Spits a glob of brown liquid onto the gravel. Then he runs his hand along the bumper and mumbles, "Well, 'least there ain't much damage." I nod. For a moment, it seems like the situation is going to resolve without further incident. Then the woman pulls a cigarette from her purse and lights it up, right there next to her son. She inhales deeply and exhales a gray cloud through her nose. The cloud wafts into the baby's face along with the gray whiffs spiraling off the glowing end of the cigarette. The baby blinks, rubs his nose, obviously irritated. Evan and I are just standing there, totally dumbfounded, unable to comprehend the negligence we're witnessing. First no car seat. Now this. What in the hell.

But here's where our opinions diverge, where I don't agree with Evan at all. Because the next thing he says, after taking the dip out of his mouth and flicking it on the ground, is "and you wonder why none of them act right when they grow up." Of course, I know exactly what he means by "them," as if skin color is somehow a factor, as if there aren't thousands of white women, many of whom live in this very town, who smoke cigarettes around babies on a daily basis.

This is the problem I have with Evan. The problem I have with our town in general. Why I don't always agree with the things he or other people around here say. They make it seem like if a black person does something stupid it's because of their blackness, but if a white person does something stupid it's just because they're stupid. Do you see the difference? There's a big difference. I don't think it's right, and it really makes me consider whether Evan and the other folks in this town are really that good of people after all. Even though I really want to believe in their innate goodness. Even though I really want to believe I am good myself.

Sherry Cook Stanforth

23 and Appalachian Me

Warning: I projectile
spit wherever I go,
grocery store or classroom.
Spit happens, too, on church
or state business, leaving hard
evidence of my passing.

A single tear or a wellspring
of grief, strands of my hair
wound around
a baby's fat finger,
blood streaking
public toilet seats—I continue

existing in double helixes
implying an atom, a cell, a body
system—a soul flung to star,
a blooming multiverse.
Each day, I rise ready
to mark my territory.

Now, here's a chance to further
expand *me* in one lick. How tempting
to prove my Isles spark burns wild
or that my cheekbones are indeed
Cherokee—that I can be *more*,
holding rights to wander specific

ridges or shores while crooning
ancestral tunes—or justifying
some hotheaded German streak
I'm inclined to ignore. One touch
of my tongue to paper, seal up
the data, send it off…then wait

a few weeks for the key to me.
Yet, a friend just learned that he's
Neanderthal dumb, and another—
not one shred of Irish luck
despite the red hair. An alt-white
family I know posted how

they're practically quadroon
(Virginia born, the supreme kind)
while some other folks swept away
shards of a God-awful ruinous truth.
I guess with 23, you don't always
like what you see.

Dishing out spit may bring
nothing but trouble.
Two centuries into
eternal sleep, I could be
cloned for my curls
or framed by my own DNA.

Who will lay claim to
faith inside
this promised land,
and who is
bound to be
shot down?

The bits and pieces left behind
wait to be defined. Time and again,
we claim we must break
people free of chains—
yet, the same old spit keeps
right on happening.

Michael Thompson

Ascent

Oil, Charcoal, and Gold Leaf in Canvas (48"x64")

Jerry Buchanan
Song of the Stones

I.
We are stones in the valley, on the mountain,
and underground—round, dense, rough, hard,
smooth, jagged. Dirt and grass claim us as kin.
We lie in dust and mud in heaps and seams,

sometimes alone—worn by rain, wind, sun—
assured our place. From eons past, we exist
beyond boredom and despair. Without knowing
or feeling, our molecules vibrate and wait.

II.
The other day a boy skimmed a flat rock
on a watery surface, and rumors of the lifting
stirred subterranean fissures. Metamorphic
shufflers sing of levitation, of the near day

someone lifts us. Smug in obvious accuracy,
others claim gravity as god. Local gossip stirs
fear that shifting how things lie will lead
to molten uprisings exploding like hot lava.

III.
Most stones forget about the ripples on the dark
blue, shimmered mirror. Common sense reckons
water-skipping bouncers settle on the bottom
of the lake among the sand, fish, and algae.

A few of us sedimentary hopefuls still hang out on the ledge. If we fall, will our dense structure change? Now and then, knowing comes unexpectedly—
    in a rumble from below.

John Thomas York
Soul Bus

Every school bus has a large rear-view mirror between windshield and ceiling, big enough to allow the driver to see most of the passengers. At first, I could only imagine leering faces looking back at me, smart-ass children popping gum and throwing spit wads. The first person I saw clearly was the dreaded Mr. Hatcher, trainer of bus drivers, wearing a narrow-brimmed hat—a short man with a deep voice, a hill-country accent. My older cousins who received their training from the man said Hatcher was a tough customer. And I was an inexperienced driver: I was sixteen and had not driven a vehicle with manual transmission. In 1970, all of the buses were stick shift.

I didn't really want to take the wheel, especially the first bus, a rattletrap Chevrolet. It had a grim grill of a mouth, vents in the hood that looked like nostrils, just the kind of bus to give small children nightmares. It smelled of years of dirt, no matter how much anybody swept it out or mopped it down, and the seats were covered in cracking plastic. The clutch was just about worn out; starting on a hill, I stalled two or three times before attaining forward momentum.

I didn't really want to be a bus driver. I didn't want to get up at six and be on the road by seven, gathering a load of noisy kids. And bus drivers were second-class citizens in the world of high school. For one thing, we couldn't play sports—unable to make it back to campus in time for practice. Jocks were at the top of the heap. (I had already failed at basketball and football.) For another thing, we were mostly poor kids who needed the work.

I needed a job. The summer before eleventh grade the

best I could do was a gig driving my uncle's tractor in August when he harvested tobacco. Afflicted with eczema on my fingers, I could not do the more lucrative job of "priming," or pulling the leaves. I drove a tractor hauling a long, narrow cart through the field as Uncle Money and sons bent over and harvested the prime leaf. We always started at sunrise. By noon I made twelve dollars maybe.

I needed money to buy a new guitar and a two-hundred-watt amplifier so my cousins and I could have a respectable band, so we could get gigs on weekends playing for dances. We lacked the wattage necessary to stir adolescents to get up and boogie to the beat. We also needed a bass player and a lead singer.

That summer before my junior year, my mother, for her part, had had it with me bumming money. She told me to go over to the county bus garage and sign up for training. I would be a school bus driver.

I never thought about what I might learn from the experience.

Everyone who drove a school bus in Yadkin County had to first receive instruction from Mr. Glen Hatcher. On the first morning of training, we novice drivers gathered at the garage and joined our instructor on a bus. After a lecture on how to shift from first to second to third and fourth, Mr. Hatcher said it was time to drive on the road.

Later, I thought I was doing pretty well, getting to fourth gear—cruising down a two-lane black top, enjoying the pastoral scenery—when Hatcher stood up and shouted, "God damn it! Slow this bus down! Do you think this is the Charlotte Motor Speedway?"

The next morning, I was driving when Mr. Hatcher

decided to test my powers of concentration. He beat time on the metal wall of the bus as he sang, "Bringing in the sheaves, / Bringing in the sheaves, / We shall come rejoicing/ Bringing in the sheaves!"

Somehow, I passed the training and got a license. In August, the principal of the elementary school, Mr. Albert Martin, offered me a bus route, one that included a swing through Barney Hill, the Black community. I didn't really have any choice. If I said no, Mama would hear it right away. (She taught third grade at Boonville, Mr. Martin's school.) She had probably lobbied for me. The faces in the rear-view mirror began to take shape, a few white faces, but mostly faces that were different shades of brown. And my face, wondering how this new job would turn out.

By the time we got to October, Old #35 was retired, recycled into sardine cans, probably. I was assigned New #35, a shiny bus, untouched by dirt, sweat, soda pop, or vomit. That shiny condition would not last long, of course, but I and my riders enjoyed the newness. The bus had boxy corners and a tinted windshield. It was easy to launch out of first gear, even on the steepest part of Barney Hill, so no child was inspired to lose his or her Fruit Loops.

All of the drivers kept their busses parked at their homes. In the morning, I walked out of Grandma's house carrying my books and binder and climbed up the steps of the bus. By 7:00, I was rolling down the gravel driveway and onto Rockford Road.

I turned from Rockford onto Nebo Road, a curving road without hills or dips, the old wagon road to Winston-Salem. Heading east, facing the dawn, I said a quick prayer, asking God to keep me out of the creeks and ditches, asking that I cause no harm to any child, either intentionally or unintentionally. Then I took a short dirt road over to Highway 67, which was as straight as yardstick and roller-coastered over the hills and dales.

I picked up a few kids on 67, but most of my charges lived in Barney Hill. I drove north, downhill, stopping for riders, and getting within sight of the Yadkin River. I picked up Bucky Tidwell and his sister. Bucky was always too sleepy to say hello. Either that, or he still remembered our rock band fiasco. Most of the youn'uns, of every age, white or Black, were quiet on the morning trip.

By the time we arrived at Boonville School, the passengers boiled over, the younger kids bubbling out the front door. The high school students talked or listened to soul music on a transistor radio or tape player. Sometimes Lane Williams sang a song. Lane was the lead singer in a band and had a good voice. He had very dark skin, and one morning he made the girls laugh when he sang, "Wash Me and I Shall Be Whiter Than Snow!"

After waiting for a few minutes for any late riders, I drove us up to Starmount High School. In all, my run took just a little over an hour.

I came to be on friendly terms with most of the riders, especially the high schoolers.

The spring of my junior year, I and my peers in Mr. McNeill's humanities seminar put together a literary magazine. On the day the magazine came out, after school, while I was sitting behind the wheel and waiting for the buses to roll, a senior named Michael Pate stopped at the open window, reached in and shook my hand, saying, "Good job, John! I like your poems!" He had many poems in the magazine, better poems than mine, and he was heading to the big time, to Wake Forest, in the fall.

Before we rode to the elementary school, a girl named Gloria borrowed my copy of the magazine, *Green Salad*, and found one of my poems. Gloria was one of the cheerleaders, a confident girl who had a commanding voice. When she said, "Listen to this," everyone paid attention:

Sunrise Service
American shouts and anthems roll
Across the Anglo-Saxon land,
The white mob's mouth
Shouts praises at a well-attended Sunrise Service:
"It is time to celebrate another victory
Under this patriotic sky. . ."
As I look up I cannot help but wonder
If the fantastic red is not the stain of a Cherokee's blood,
If the blue is not the remains of a Negro's tears,
The scattered, white clouds,
the peeling paint on a nation's face.

Gloria said, "Good poem, Johnny."

There were no adult bus drivers at Starmount, just students, but I never heard of anyone having a serious accident. So maybe my older cousins were right about Mr. Hatcher: if you could drive with him on board, you were ready for the job.

Yes, some drivers were immature kids. When I missed school for over a week, out with the flu the spring of my senior year, a younger boy named Alvin subbed for me. When I returned to school and to driving, my riders told me they were glad I was back.

"That boy would yell at us to sit down and be quiet, and would slam on the brakes when we didn't listen!"

My sub either didn't have Mr. Hatcher for training or,

if he did, he didn't listen to his strategy for getting a busload on young'uns to settle down.

When we made the afternoon run, everyone was wide awake. The high school kids mostly ignored the younger kids, who could get rowdy. When it was so loud I couldn't hear the rock 'n' roll playing in my head, when I couldn't understand anyone asking a question, I remembered Mr. Hatcher's instructions: pull over; stop the bus; pull on the emergency brake, and just sit there until everyone gets quiet.

When I used this strategy, Gloria, the cheerleader, got tired of sitting and watching the leaves on the trees changing color; she turned around and shouted, "Shit, now! Get quiet, or I'm going to set your butts out on the side of the road!"

When her high school buddies joined in the harangue, order was restored.

"Okay, Mr. Big Stuff," she sneered, turning back to the front. "You can take us home now."

What if I could reach through the rear-view mirror hanging above my head? What if I could crawl through and visit that time? Could I be a more courageous boy?

One afternoon while I was driving from Starmount to Boonville Elementary—before the younger kids' chattering covered up conversations—the girls were talking about dating. I looked up to the mirror when somebody said, "I bet Johnny York would date a Black girl if he took a chance." She grinned at me and I grinned back, but I didn't say anything. I didn't want to talk about the reasons why it wouldn't happen. (Looking back, I am sure these girls were frustrated, going to a school where they were probably related to most of the Black guys, and the rest of the boys were off limits.)

It wasn't that I hadn't thought about dating any of these

girls: they were quite pretty, and when the cheerleaders on the bus wore their uniforms, their legs enhanced my sexual fantasy world. But if interracial dating was happening at Starmount, I didn't know about it. (A distinct possibility—I was rather clueless.) The only time I had seen an inter-racial couple was once when I went to the city, to a shopping center in Winston-Salem: a white girl and a Black boy, nice-looking kids, both wearing glasses, were walking by holding hands. An older white woman turned and stared at them. Her jowls and her dewlap quivered as she said, "Well, the very idea! You, white girl, let go of that boy's hand!"

They walked on, obviously mortified, ignoring her, their idealistic ship running up against an old, ugly rock.

Of course, it didn't take a scene at a shopping center to put the brakes on my romantic or hormonal impulses. Deeper down, there was the vivid memory of a Sunday at the dinner table—I must have been eight, my sister, six. Dad had found an article in the paper, a story about a campus protest at some Yankee college where, out on the lawn, Black guys were applying suntan lotion to white girls' backs, out where photographers could record the scene.

Dad told my mother, "If I had a daughter who did such a thing, I'd take my pistol and shoot her and the black bastard both!"

I found Daddy's outburst frightening. What was the problem?

My passengers on #35 knew more about prejudice than I did, of course, and, listening to them, I learned about some of its cruel ironies. One day, making a stop in Barney Hill, I saw a white woman sitting in a parked car. She looked like she had been crying. One of the older girls on the bus told how this woman was married to a Black man, a soldier, and, when he brought her home to introduce her to his family, his mama would not speak to the girl. The mother didn't want any white people in her house, especially some trashy girl whose parents would allow mixing of the races.

Integration happened in the Yadkin County Schools in 1966 when I was in seventh grade. My sister had a Black teacher, and there were three Black guys in my class, boys whose parents had volunteered them to go to Boonville School: the county's all-Black school would remain in operation for another year.

I could not see how the Black boys were inferior to their white peers. Indeed, they were rather quiet at first and always attentive to the lessons. Looking at their brown faces and seeing how they interacted with teachers and students, I decided that my father was wrong. These boys were just folks.

Generally speaking, there wasn't the rabidly racist tone in Yadkin County that was found in the Deep South. And at school, there were no ugly scenes like the ones we saw on TV. There were no bomb threats called in to the schools—as happened in Greensboro and Charlotte.

Perhaps that's why my cousins and I thought, when I was in eighth grade, we could recruit Bucky Tidwell for our little combo—we had two guitars and drums, and he was the bass player we needed. He lived only five minutes from Bernard and Patsy's house, where we practiced in the basement. But when Uncle Bernard found out that we had invited a Black person to his house, he angrily put a stop to it, a surprise and a disappointment.

I had the job of calling Bucky and letting him know the rehearsal was off. I must have been too honest about the reason why, for my mother chastised me: "Don't you think you could be more tactful? Consider his feelings!"

A quiet boy, Bucky never had much to say to me after our rehearsal fell through.

In 1971, a junior taking American history, I was beginning to understand more about the legacy of racism. And, sometimes, just listening to my passengers, I learned things I hadn't thought about before. I heard them talk about promises made to the Black students on the verge of integration, promises never kept. At Starmount, they did not have the same opportunities for positions of leadership and responsibility that they would have had at their old school. At their new school, even if they voted as a block, the African-American students made up less than ten percent of the student body. And they didn't have the sense of community they enjoyed before, or opportunities for the maintaining of traditions.

I just assumed that all Blacks were in favor of integration. A liberal Appalachian kid, I assumed that, once integration happened, the fight was over—there was nothing more to discuss. But I began to see that the issue was more complicated than I had imagined. It was not until I was much older that I came to consider the Black community's relatively small size. Living in pockets in Jonesville, Boonville, Barney Hill, East Bend, and Yadkinville, the Blacks in Yadkin County, in Appalachia, were easy to ignore, easy to dismiss. They were not seen as a threat, as in the Deep South, but were they treated as equals?

In the early seventies, change was sneaking around corners, getting airtime on the radio. One Friday afternoon, while we were on the run from Starmount to the elementary school, the cheerleaders were wearing their uniforms, blue and burnt orange. There had been a pep rally, and there would be a home basketball game that night. Somebody turned up a tape player: when Jean Knight started singing "Mr. Big Stuff," four or five girls stood up and danced in unison in the aisle, all facing the right-hand side of the bus and shaking their butts. They were goddesses proclaiming victory over every Mr. Big Stuff in the world—every over-stuffed male ego, every ladies' man put in his place, and (Keep it up, girls!) every stuffed shirt, every stiff full of stuff, every crude and countrified cracker who ever shouted something ugly: "Who do you think you are?"

Looking in the rear-view mirror, I saw that their dancing was not safe, for several reasons, certainly against the rules, but it was steady as she goes. I didn't tell them to stop. Maybe Don Cornelius had his *Soul Train*, but I was driving the *Soul Bus*. No speeding, no slamming on the brakes: just an easy ride as the girls bounced to the next song, Sly and the Family Stone (the Mothers and Fathers of Integrated Cool, the Righteous Sisters and Brothers of Fiery Funk, the Funka-mechanix of the New Generation) singing, "Thank You (Falletenme Be Mice Elf Agin)"!

Alexandra McIntosh

Walking the Railroad Tracks With Brian Wilson

All afternoon, spring birds busy themselves in honeysuckle bushes. We riff off each other's ideas, memories just beneath the surface like the gar gathered around the bridge's pilings, the river just below the bluff. We come upon the dried-out body of a fox, its meaty insides scraped clean, fur stretched tight along paws and spine.

When I was young I was scared of my skeleton, I say, looking ahead to where the tracks curve into the trees. Brian doesn't say anything, so I continue. *I'd lie in bed thinking about it under my skin, wrapped in muscle and tissue.*

Brian bends down to pick up a rail spike. We like the mangled ones, their sharp curves and edges thrown into the gravel. *Trains are ghosts,* Brian says, *their whistles and rattles haunt the landscape.*

You should write that down, I say, half teasing. A patch of trout lilies appears along the wood's edge. *My grandma had high cheekbones— I could hardly look at them, the thick white mineral underneath, the pockets of marrow.*

I know something about haunting, he says seriously, referring to the voices. I nod and catch his glance with my own. *When I was young, I thought I was possessed,* I say quietly. The intrusive thoughts, the dark cloud over my eyes. *It still scares me.*

Do the skeletons of trees haunt the leaves? Brian asks, looking up at a bone-white sycamore. *Or the other way around? Are we the ghosts?*

Thomas Alan Holmes
Bristol, TN/VA

Well, dang!
Big Bang
of Country Twang:
Carters sang,
bent a string,
then a gang
craved a tang
of something fine,
purest shine.
Engines rang,
bringing swallers
one distills
in the hills
and the hollers,
lawman follows
like the races
thunder ridden
in the hidden
routes and traces,
catch as catch can,
Appalachian
tale or riddle,
down the middle,
mountaineer
and Volunteer,
hopeful, wistful,
concealed pistol,
lonesome whistle,
Goddamned Bristol.

Damian Dressick
The Road Still Traveled

  Shortcuts are just another way of showing you think you know better than everyone else, my father might have told me—had he been the kind of man who dispensed his wisdom in bite-sized, epigrammatic *dictums*. Not that I would have listened. Case in point: a winter's night in 1994 a friend and I were driving from Morgantown, West Virginia, to pick up a buddy from his spartan grad school apartment in Athens, Georgia. We were headed for New Orleans, a place I was moving to for the expressed purposes of heavy drinking and other forms of misbehavior.

  These were the days before Google maps or cell phones or GPS of any sort. Reliance on the Rand McNally Road Atlas and good judgment was simply how all interstate travel was managed. In possession of one of the two, we were able to discern on page 167 an off-kilter Cy Twombly of thin blue lines beckoning us over the mountains with the promise of cutting off a sizable chunk of tedious highway mileage. My friend and I nodded to one another, smug as tv preachers. We knew best. We were putting one over on every last bumper-to-bumper sucker growing old on I-77.

  Like most bad decisions, the choice looked like a good one—right up until we were too far along to do anything other than follow it through to conclusion. We assumed there would be signage. We assumed there would be pavement. We assumed the roads we came across had some likelihood of appearing on our map. We mistakenly believed errors in navigation could be undone by turning the car around without backing up hundreds of yards of narrow cliffside path lacking the benefit of guard rail. We thought a 1/4 tank of gas would be enough to comfortably get across the Allegheny Ridge and back to the interstate. We did not count on steady drizzle or fog assiduous as judgment.

Eventually, of course, we arrived in Georgia—eighteen hours late, but no punches traded. We drank whiskey and talked books with our host. Then we all headed on to City That Care Forgot, where things went as they will go in a place like New Orleans before the wheels inevitably come off. But as Arlo Guthrie says about picking up the garbage outside of Stockbridge, Massachusetts—that's not what I'm here to talk about.

Writing anything that smacks of memoir invariably means interrogating one's experiences, and getting this snake-bit road trip on the page is no different. But penning this particular clusterfuck demands little untangling of false remembrance or dispensing with later mythologizing to discover what *really* happened. It simply isn't that kind of story. As much as one might want, or occasionally need, to imagine the act of writing as an elixir that bestows magical powers to erode the layers of ego, and time and bullshit that stand in the way of some Eldorado of real *truth*, that's just not a going concern here. As it so often happens—and we are so rarely inclined to admit—what truth there is sits right up there on the surface, floating like a morning after pill in a bull shot. This was just *another* time, out of a whole lot of them, that I thought I knew better—that rules, immutable as gravity or compound interest—didn't apply. The trip was a minor screw up in the nesting doll set of mistakes that inevitably steers things—like one's twenties—into a full-on jumble. After all, when you can't stop cutting every corner, the mere knowledge you're inclined that way isn't worth the moonlight behind the clouds on a West Virginia night lost in the rain.

LuLu Johnson
Paso Fino

One horse lived off Coffee Road. She was a Paso Fino, the type with fancy gaits that can only be engaged by a rider who knows where to press his thighs and knees, when to grip his shins and release, how tap his heels and lay the reins along her neck to make her show out, strut and prance. But this boy didn't know any of that.

The summer I graduated high school, the boy borrowed this horse from a friend. The night before my family headed back to Texas, he drove me north away from the lake. He turned right onto what wasn't a busy two-lane. Two miles east of town, he turned left. That's where the woman lived, in a trailer parked on Coffee Road. Her mare stood at the fence patient as fate, wearing only a bridle and reins. She didn't need much. That's how good a horse she was.

Good enough to take him and me without question through the gate at the far end of the field, across what are now driveways leading back to subdivisions. That night, there was only long grass and a stream the good horse stepped smartly through for the boy who knew nothing.

That boy, we called him Kermit because of his face, took the horse and me farther east, a quarter mile to the foreclosed golf course. We thought nothing of riding across its empty tee boxes, down long sloping fairways, and across putting greens. Above us, summer cried its heart out as dusk came down that slow July way it has, black ink swirled into blue water.

I imagine the horse liked those surfaces, that the bentgrass greens felt soft as shag carpet beneath her hooves. I think she bowed her graceful neck to crop the rough because Kermit didn't know how to keep her up, that she felt him shift behind me to bump his cock against my rump. I fancy that she felt me lean away, way up into her mane to escape the pressure. Or not.

The ride didn't last long. The lady in the trailer had said Kermit must bring the horse right straight back because he'd ruin her if he rode too long. She might've said the same for me. But she knew nothing of the coming thing, the horse or the lady.

Neither of them knew that my virginity had become a burden I wanted shed of like a tight lace dress that itched my neck. They didn't know this, but Kermit did.

Kermit knew so well that when he took me home that night, he didn't take me right straight there. Knew well enough to cross the top of Shady Lane and veer left at the start of the logging road where that too-big house now sits. Knew well enough to back his Gremlin deep into a tunnel of trees where cicadas screamed syncopated love songs above our heads while I lost my virginity like a sneeze. The kind that hurts your throat.

The kind that makes you lean your head against a Mercury Marquis backseat window the next day and watch Mississippi spiral by outside like a movie. A movie in which the character feels changed in a deeply interior way that no one in the car notices. It was that kind of sex.

The kind that makes a girl look back with regret, the kind that makes her tell her very first college boyfriend she wished she'd saved herself for him, as if her hymen were a roll of Lifesavers, a flavor he might like. Peppermint. Butterscotch. Or not.

It was the kind of sex that turns my head when I drive home from riding lessons now that I live here. The kind that all these years later makes me glance right at the mildewed trailer and conjure the woman who loaned her mare. But neither are there, and her once-lovely pasture has filled with invasive trash trees and rusted cars on cinder blocks. A lone billy goat tries to crop the hillside clear, but he fails. Miserably. I drive west fast, but even so, I see no horses there.

Speeding past, it occurs to me that that summer night forty years ago, I saw the white trailer in its heyday, met the woman at her prime, rode the fancy horse at her finest, fucked Kermit at his teenage apex. The other day, his son died.

Such a tragedy makes me want to rewind the tape—not to those moments in his hatchback beneath screaming cicadas to regain my innocence, but farther back than that, back to the horse on the golf course.

There, I return to rub my butt purposefully against his front, reveal my desire in that way. I press my heels and cluck my tongue and get the horse to stop. I slide off her slick sides and hold out my hand to him. He drops down lightly beside me on the third tee overlooking a narrow stream choked with boulders.

There I let him lower himself onto me atop that mattress-soft Bermuda grass box. With the good horse cropping leisurely behind us, I expose my open knees. I lower my defenses, my prudent resistance. I set aside my blasé charade and unmask my deepest sympathy. Smiling, I offer the young man the best of what I had at that tender age to give. I give it to him with a surfeit of lust in that fragile and wrenching moment we became us.

In that dream, I reach up and stroke his chubby cheek. I stare past the dark bags beneath his wet brown eyes and linger my kiss longer on his pudgy lower lip. Relaxing back, I allow him to feel he puts me through my paces, rides well enough to command ecstasy in response.

In that dream when he does what he didn't, I do things I didn't.

That time, I tender more than just my itchy innocence. I see clear past his shroud of imperfections to his crushing future fate and gift the guy his best young moment.

That time in this dream, I look up and speak. That time, I call his name. I say, *Ken*.

Llewellyn McKernan
Appalachian Love Song

My girl's a blossom of rye, by gum.
She's a sweep of the narrow,
the wide of the fun,
she's a blamed carat diamond
stacked with sun.

She's the shadow in the shade,
the warm love stone,
a berry-blue bird,
the mountain in the crumb:
a toss-a-hat, cake-walk,
rainbow-dawn.

She's the whiz
of a whistle,
a sunset-on-the run,
the hairshirt princess
of happy outcomes.

She's a kick-a-poo
joy-juice lady, Ta-Dum.
She's a boogie-
woogie crone,
down to
the bone.

Laurie Wilcox-Meyer

Dearest Mother,

I can't hear black bear on the sidewalk.
She doesn't alarm me.
But whoa to 24/7 promenade of false facts.
The rift of drowning dreams a universe wide.
Instead of bees, poisoned yacks and
tweets swarming.
We place mountain lion and coyote in cities.
Thank you for plenty, mycelia's worldwide web.
And I want to crawl into black bear's cave.
There in darkness mystery's light.

A. Riel Regan

Belief in the City

There are people who believe in this city.
That this city can be better.

During my drive to work I pass a couple giving out fresh vegetables,
and a black man holding a sign for a *Stop Killing Us* walk.
I've shopped at farmers markets, but not lately.
I've marched before, but not recently.
I've done river sweeps and park sweeps and
I pick up litter when I see it
but I've not done city sweeps,
I wonder, why bother?

But during my drive home, there they are;
across the street from artless and angry graffiti scrawl of
CPD DIST 4 = KKK
and down the street from halfway houses
and a new community center
and several beloved old chapels,

and there they are;
teenagers and twenty-somethings twenty-something strong
picking up trash on Reading
and the next day, the block was once again cluttered with trash
but it was less.

But it was less.

Judy Jenks
Trailer Park Chicks

I had never lived in a trailer park before and knew nothing about trailer park etiquette. The irritable trailer park manager who lived 4 trailers over had little etiquette at all. But, the burly man had rules.

I can't tell you the number of times I had to move my car because the front end was hanging over the edge of the gravel parking spot. "It'll kill the grass," he'd grumble. You shoulda' seen his face turn red when my boyfriend came over in his oversized pick-up truck and parked wherever he pleased.

"You gotta' move your truck!" he'd shout over the rumble of engine and tailpipes. My boyfriend complied by moving his truck about a foot. This would go on a few times before the trailer park manager would huff back over to his own single wide trailer madder than the entire C ward of the local mental hospital.

Little did this guy know I was incubating chicks in my trailer park bathroom. A constant chirping, scratching and scurrying came from behind that closed door. If startled, there were a few seconds of a peeping riot, then they'd settle back to a gentle scratching ruckus. I must have had 35 chicks in that bathroom at any given time. And I only had one bathroom.

I admit, I had a little difficulty assimilating myself to trailer park life. Perhaps the rescued recliner that wouldn't recline didn't look so refined on the porch. Just maybe the Harley Davidson hubcap hammered to the side of the trailer didn't help to elevate the station of the trailer park itself. Who knew I shouldn't hang my wash on the porch railing? Mr Trailer Park Manager hurried toward me with foamy spittle spraying his left cheek wheezing "Naw, Naw, Naw! I told you there's no clothes lines in this trailer park!"

That day, I was in no mood for his meddling mania and faced him with unladylike utterings on my tongue ready to tell him what he could do with his clothesline criteria, but then... I heard the chicks. A pandemonium of peeps went from zero to 60 in three seconds or less, and intensified. I warily watched as his head cocked to the left and he stared at me like a banty rooster sizing up his competition.

I stared back, then hooked the door with my foot and pushed it shut, dampening the sounds of the contraband fowl. His eyes wavered and he broke the staredown without a word. To my surprise he turned and left the porch. That's the first time I saw him a little off balance.

Nevertheless, he continued to soldier his way into my business. I would see him lurking near my trailer as if monitoring for misconduct. I figured my music was his misery. He frequently fussed, futilely, because it was the one thing I wouldn't give up. Apparently, he did not like Merle Haggard because every time I put on a Merle Haggard record he showed up at my door, "Your music's too loud!" Every. Single. Time.

One evening I drove to the local bar looking forward to a leisurely reprieve. Not long after my first drink a friend waved at me and said, "Hey, I just drove by your place to see if you were home—did you know the police are at your trailer?"

"What?"

"Yeah, I was just there, and your trailer's surrounded by police," he said, half amused because I could make no further noise come out of my open mouth.

I had no idea what this could be about but quickly drove to the trailer park and sure enough, two police cars and an ambulance were parked in front of my trailer. I left my car in the road and weaved my way through the wave of garish lights and spied the trailer park manager lying on my trailer park porch, his face partially obscured by rusty blood.

I stepped back, thinking it best to keep my distance for a few minutes.

I found my boyfriend handcuffed in the back seat of a police car. He had a grin on his face no doubt fueled by the empty Jack Daniels bottle I spotted lying by his truck. He seemed no worse for the altercation and after a few fits and starts I was able to piece together a story; it seems my boyfriend had violated major rules of the trailer park by parking on the grass and, to add insult, he cranked up the volume of Merle Haggard singing, "I Think I'll Just Stay Here and Drink."

The trailer park manager had blustered over and rashly repeated trailer park rules to a somewhat inebriated country boy used to living in wide open spaces. Stern words turned to yelling, gesticulating to fists flying, a knocked-out trailer park manager to a 911 call, all which led to this scene before me.

I was standing by the police car considering all this when I heard a familiar voice yelling "Naw, Naw! Stop!" I spied the trailer park manager being strapped to a stretcher, struggling, his arm extended and an index finger pointing me out like I was already in a line up at the police station. "There she is! That's her!" A policeman waved me over with his notebook. As I got close to the stretcher I braced for the Manager's wrath. But instead, he looked a little frightened.

The policeman turned to me and said, very matter of factly, "He says you're a spy."

For the second time that night I was bewildered beyond words. I turned back to the stretcher to see the trailer park manager looking at me, eyes wide. He slowly nodded his head at me and whispered, "I heard it." Out of the corner of my mouth I whispered back, "Heard what?"

He raised his head off the pillow, "The radio …" his eyes narrowed "…you have a covert high frequency two-way radio in your trailer." He was staring at me earnestly like I was secret intelligence for the FBI. Like I was translating movements into classified encrypted messages. Like I copied clandestine coordinates for unidentified underground organizations. Me, an agent for anarchy.

Third time tonight, I'm speechless.

I realized the policeman looked a little amused as he talked into his shoulder and called over his partner. She walked into the rotating light and handed me an armful of chicks in a box. The quiet birds erupted into a raucous round of high-pitched peeping that quickly settled to low rolling chirps.

I glanced at the man tied to the stretcher. He was concentrating on those feathered fowl and as recognition turned to realization his whole body reacted violently. He started straining at the straps, Naw! Nawww! What!!! What the he!!? You have CHICKENS! … in your trailer?? Nawwwwwww…"

And it went on. A damning derecho of dirty words. I cradled the chicks and strode away quickly, listening to his litany of foul language fade as he was loaded into the ambulance. I decided to check on my boyfriend. As I neared the police car, I noticed he wasn't smiling and his face looked a little white. "You okay?" I asked. He looked up at me with suspicion and said, "They say you're a spy".

Eugene Stevenson
Heart's Code

We kill it off, slowly, in circles of
work, travel, family visits, talk it to death in
bed before we sleep, before we make
each other gasp. It does not just die.

What was her name? the wife asked.
Memory, the husband answered.
What was the hotel? she kept knitting.
A ghost town, he counted needle clicks.

Did anybody know? she pressed her lips.
Not even us, he labored to breathe.
No forgiveness. Why? a swallowed shout.
I don't know, I know, tapped in heart's code.

We betray it, quickly, between strange lips,
between strange legs, send it away.
It does not just die. We are accomplices, blind,
so dispatch love long before it is ready to go.

Ann Shurgin

Percussion, Mid-Pandemic

I'm out for a walk, to breathe fresh air.
Last of the fall leaves skitter down the street.
Someone comes out of the house just ahead.
I pull the mask out of my pocket, stop,
turn away, loop it around my ears,
reset my earbuds.

White porch curtains flap against the rail,
Two men sit talking, smoking; a woman joins them, lighting up.
I take the outer edge of the sidewalk, head down.
Empty garbage cans tip at the curb, lids thumping.
I pass the house, give myself 10 yards,
undo one ear loop, leave the other attached.

Bare branches fiddle-bow scratch on power lines.
Here comes the race walker, his long gray hair flying.
He inhales and blows, fueling angry exertion.
I take the other side of the street, a quick re-loop over my right ear.

Wind chimes sound every note loud as a dinner bell.
I press on, running out of sidewalk;
nod to a bearded dog walker; cross the street again.
Laughter erupts, staccato, from an open window.
I reach the school, walk faster to beat the dismissal bell.
Parents lined up in cars sit idle, windows down.

Two more blocks, up the hill, and I round the corner to my backyard.
Inside, I lock the door, unmask, breathe, look outside, listen.

The percussion of a windy day rises, in crescendo,
as the sky darkens and the timpani thunder in.

Anna Egan Smucker
Not What He Expected

The year St. Paul's bulged beyond breaking,
my fourth grade class was exiled
to a narrow room across the street,
former home of *The Shamrock Bar*.

Filing in the back door, we ducked
the blast of greasy exhaust
from Bulka's Grill next door.
Inside, forty of us in four long rows
faced Sister Mary Benedict.
"I have eyes in the back of my head,"
she told us, and we saw them
unblinking through the black veil.

Once a man knocked at the never-used front door,
asked, "Where's the bar? *The Shamrock?*"
Informed that it was now St. Paul's Annex,
he peered at us, the chalkboard, crucifix,
statue of Mary, the cheap striped rug,
and rubbed his eyes, a Rip Van Winkle
wondering what happened to the beer,
friends *here* just last night,
the banter, clink of glass,
ether of the stale, sweet air.

Thomas E. Strunk
A History of the Masks I Wore

There are four. There are others of course, lying about, but they aren't very useful. No, there are only four masks I ever wear.

My wife makes the first one herself. In early March 2020, she sews it out of my old flannel shirts, inserting a piece of foil at the top to keep it in place and stitching black bands that stretch over my ears. The front is sky blue crisscrossed with red, black, and orange horizontal and vertical lines. The back is yellow and black.

My wife is a nurse. We are lucky. She teaches at the university. At the hospital, nurses and doctors are working long shifts in PPE, exposing themselves to the virus; some are sleeping in their cars rather than exposing their families to the lethal virus. Some will catch COVID; others will leave the profession unable and unwilling to endure the trauma, suffering, and long hours.

Although healthcare leaders provide mixed messages about the effectiveness of masks in these early days of the pandemic when they are hard to find, my wife retreats upstairs and sews masks for me, our twin daughters, and our neighbors. I am grateful because poor scientist that I am, even I know a face covering is better protection against COVID than walking out into the world defenseless. Besides, it is heavy and warm for the cold days and masks my face well and the uncertainty it carries.

My one daughter has a cough and a fever that has lasted several days. The World Health Organization has just determined that the coronavirus has reached pandemic levels.

My wife worries our daughter may have COVID. She has had asthma and bronchitis and goes every year to the doctor or emergency room for some lung related ailment. In time, we will learn that COVID somehow generally spares young children, but we don't know that yet, and even still it won't be every child. Instead, we worry what COVID could do to her.

"I'm calling the school to let them know I think she has COVID."

"She doesn't have COVID," I tell my wife, skeptical as usual.

"Well, she has been out of school for a couple of days, and her cough isn't going away. I'm taking her in."

So my wife and daughter head to the emergency room at the children's hospital. My other daughter and I head out to do the grocery shopping. When we arrive at the Kroger, the parking lot is a riotous beehive. Every parking spot is taken; cars are crammed into no-parking spaces, and some are being towed. We idle through the rows of cars until one pulls out and we get our space.

We find one of the few carts left, head inside, and wend our way down the aisles crowded with people but empty of many items. The canned-soup section is decimated. The pasta shelves bare except for the low-carb veggie-pasta. No toilet paper, a couple packs of tissues. An anxiety creeps among us, unaccustomed to such scarcity.

My wife texts that they do not have COVID tests available at the children's hospital. I can feel the fear behind her message. Not only may we not know if our daughter has COVID, but also one of the best hospitals in the country is unprepared. The pandemic began months ago across the ocean, and we did nothing except wait in denial that it would ever come here. We have no masks, no tests, and even more no common will to resist the virus. The election year is training us to distrust each other. We are exposed to all that is coming our way.

We get in a check-out line that stretches halfway down the shopping aisle. I text my wife back: "The grocery store is wild. We'll be here a while. Keep me posted." We inch forward with our carts.

The woman ahead of me turns and says, "This is crazy. They should have more workers. I'm shopping for a funeral gathering. They say we shouldn't be getting together like this, but there ain't no way we're listening to them. My uncle died and we're getting together for him. I don't care what they say."

I nod and look to my phone. I have received a text from my brother-in-law, a financial planner, telling us, "The markets are reeling. You probably want to have some cash on hand."

Another text announces that all Ohio schools are shutting down and going online for three weeks beginning Tuesday. I feel as if the anxiety of the world is wrapping itself around the anxiety in the grocery store as I wait helplessly in the slowly moving line, which now stretches to the back of the store.

We have been here for three hours, and at last it is our time to check out. We load our groceries into the van and drive down to the dollar store at the other end of the plaza to look for toilet paper and tissues. We grab what we need and get in the line that snakes through the store. Unlike Kroger where panic had a voice, here no one speaks, and a grim silence holds us.

We pay and head to the nearby ATM where I withdraw some cash. We stop to fill up the van with gas and make it back home before my wife and daughter, although our trip has taken nearly four hours door to door.

My daughter and I put away the groceries and wait for news from the hospital as the evening grows late. An email alerts me that my university has extended spring break for a week and cancelled face to face classes for the rest of the semester. Finally, my wife sends an update, "H1N1 – at the pharmacy, will be home soon." Though H1N1 is no walk in the park, we are relieved to know that our daughter has been diagnosed with something other than COVID.

When my wife and daughter arrive, we greet them with a hero's welcome, glad to be together again. We remember to check the messages on the landline and learn that the girls' school will be shutting down after tomorrow, a day earlier than the rest of the district because of a possible COVID case in the community. We aren't sure it's us, but we suspect we are responsible for getting the school closed down. We are weary and ready to hide out from the world for a while. We are going into lockdown, but mentally we are already there.

Early in the first summer of the pandemic, I receive in the mail a face mask from a local community that supports cancer patients. I send this organization money every month because they were helpful to us when my wife was diagnosed with breast cancer a few years back. And so they send us masks, which I wear. It comes with their logo and branding on it, the only branded face covering I wear during the pandemic. The mask is all white cotton. On the right side, in black ink, is the group's name, above it a red half-sunburst, below it the names of the regions they serve—Greater Cincinnati- Northern Kentucky. It is light, great for warmer weather and for indoors. In fact, I wear this mask more than any other during the pandemic. It is handy and can be easily stuffed into a pocket.

I wear this mask into my office at work and into the grocery store, the only places I go regularly anymore. We now buy our eggs and bottles of wine while people all around us are dying by the thousands. We wait desperately for a vaccine while others are being intubated at the hospitals and lying on stretchers in the hallways. People are dying alone in nursing homes and in ICU wards.

COVID has taken many forms and sown division everywhere it has traveled, one of its most pernicious qualities. People are protesting because their children need to wear masks in school. While we argue about freedom and who is an essential worker, people continue to die in hospital hallways alone.

There is one mask so essential for my work that I never even wash it, my white mask. I keep it hidden from my wife, who likes to track down dirty masks and throw them in the washer where they disappear for days. I picked up this mask, the only one I purchased, at the hardware store. I use it for every class I teach for two years. It is loose enough for me to be able to speak without constantly readjusting it, yet stiff enough to move it up from the bottom easily. The design is simple—stretchy, thin bands that fit over the ears, the lining soft cotton. There is a small band of foil to fit it to the nose, but barely noticeable, and I wear it as if there is no top and no bottom. Unlike the others, this mask I always keep neatly folded in half, just as it was sewn, and tucked safely into my bag and stored inside a plastic zip-lock wrapper that I borrow from another mask. I wear it only on the occasions when I have to speak formally in front of others, most commonly when I am teaching, the only activity where I see people face to face, or rather mask to mask.

Teaching and learning at all levels, and work for almost everyone, has become a slog—teaching on Zoom, teaching with half the class in the room and the other half on Zoom, teaching with everyone crowded into the room and always with masks and always accompanied by the fear of getting sick, of your students getting sick and dying. I tell my students, "The goal for this semester is to survive," and I mean it. I do not care if my students remember what I teach them, in fact I prefer that they live long enough to forget it.

People have lost jobs—or as our employers like to say, "There has been a RIF," a "reduction in force," bureaucratic shorthand Donald Rumsfeld would be proud of. So I wear my mask, like workers all over the country, not only to protect myself from disease, but also to cover an angry and bewildered expression. I insist on wearing my mask even after the mask mandates are lifted, partly because I've committed to being a late adopter on the idea of a return to normalcy, partly because I don't want to be coerced into smiling at all that we have lost.

Unlike my other masks, which are thin or have a fragility to them, my blue mask is durable. Masks are readily available now, and my wife decided to pick up a few, buying a couple in kids' sizes, though the girls generally continue to wear their home-sewn masks, and for me, one with different shades of blue in waves like water, dark navy blue to light sky blue. The mask projects the icy exterior I want and yet keeps me warm. On cold winter days it offers me comfort like a hot fire. It fits well –a soft interior and exterior lining, adjustable elastic straps, and easily folds to fit into a coat pocket. A good mask to have for a pandemic that has defeated many treatments and endured every season.

We spend almost all of our time at home anymore. Our more frequent walks have made me intimate with the streets in my neighborhood. I now notice how the sun comes over the trees later today than it did yesterday. Most of all there is the quiet. There are fewer cars on the road. My neighbors wave from their porches as I pass by; I say hello from a comfortable distance and continue on. No obligatory small talk. Silence is now acceptable.

When I was sent home from the university, I gathered as many of the books I needed as possible and I dragged them up here to the third floor of my house, an office space rarely used anymore since I bought a laptop after the girls were born. I find my desk covered with random stacks of paper, disregarded magazines, and receipts, the detritus of the years. I clear off enough space to put down my computer and some papers. I cram a used bookshelf that I found on the street into the corner behind me. Still not enough space for all the books which stand in piles on the floor and rise and fall and rise again to my right and left on the desk. None of which ever show up on my Zoom screen, however much they crowd around me.

When I returned to this space, I did not realize that I was going on a pilgrimage. We think of pilgrims traveling to far off lands, but there are pilgrimages we take when we are visited by the world, as we sit still in the same place and observe what comes within our view. From here, I have found a way to write and work and watch the year move over the trees on the hillside.

Nearly every day, I have sat alone looking at that hillside and myself from a distance. In the winter, the trees dress the tops of their limbs with snow leaving the bottom of the limb bare. I did not know the trees could do such things until I became still enough to see them.

The poets, or maybe just the scholars perhaps, have invented the word for the pause of breath that typically comes five half-feet into a line of poetry, the penthemimeral caesura, and even the sixth half-foot pause, the hephthemimeral caesura. Yet I do not know that the poets or the scholars have created the word to describe these tree limbs half-coated with the winter's snow, nor the hillside covered with such trees.

I know that in this silence people are dying. There should be no rejoicing for the solitude it has taken for me to notice these things.

Kari Gunter-Seymour
"Uh-Huh, It's Your Birthday"
Digital Photography

ALLISON THORPE

The Mouth Returns to Civilization

For two years it prowled like a wild thing
Hidden behind the mask
Puckering and scowling and sneering with abandon
Letting the tongue out to wag in childish defiance
Tittering and chucking its sour breath
While the eyes charaded civility

Now the mouth must wobble its way back
Powder the fret and worry from its corners
Pink the tired lips
Let them hum voice from the sun
Whisper in someone's ear
Usher the mouth out for a spin
Taking the slow curves to smile

Dick Westheimer

There Are No Maskless Men Standing in Line at the Local Pharmacy

I must have flipped
some unseen switch,

made the man jitter like ripsaw teeth
dragged along a gravel road—

he's maskless in a masked world
and I prod him to cover up

or back off. He erupts:
I've god damn had enough!

No COVID's gonna keep me down
cause it's all overblown

and I ain't done nothing wrong.
I AM OK,

it's all y'all who's sick.
It's not me, never was.

I back away, he sprays:
You're all pussies but I'm OK

I AM OK and fucking tired of all this
COVID shit. I am so damn tired. So tired.

And 'though my fear's a haze, I see
he wears a mask.

It's one that covers some scar
my scolding's rubbed raw,

and all I'd done was feed
some fire already raging.

I knew better. I must have,
but I'd baited him anyway.

What kind of man pokes a caged bear?
   I guess my kind—

whose wheedling need to preach
needs to be unmasked.

Chuck Stringer
This Year

> *Do not be afraid—I will save you.*
> *I have called you by name—you are mine.*
> —Isaiah 43:1

In this year of the virus, today I wake dreaming
of sparrows. I'd dreamed them through the redbud
and black walnut out by 2nd Bridge, and they'd
each shared their singular songs: *chipping, swamp,
white-crowned, American tree*. I lie here in bed
awhile with Memory and listen, then we walk back
to a June afternoon just below Two-Stair Crossing
to watch a bird with a brown-streaked belly hop
from rock to rock bobbing its tail and snatching gnats.
(Back home, I'd looked it up in the guide, *Louisiana
waterthrush*.) Yes, in an October of COVID-19, I reach
out to Memory and relive that chance encounter—
one bird, one man, and less than five grand minutes
connected by the creek. We all walk a little farther
downstream where a rush of July and August friends
fly in to greet us: ducks, herons, woodpeckers,
wood-warblers, mimics, and jays. Sitting up, but not
quite out of bed, I think ahead to another COVID day:
how I'll stand by the front door, pull on my Mucks,
put on my mask, pick up my walking stick, and head
for the creek hopeful in the thought that, with distance
and luck, I'll keep hearing the name *Chuck* this year.

Karla Linn Merrifield
And So On

And is a coyote word, quick to shapeshift,
tricking itself out in &, &, &—
an ampersand disguise in sand & sandstone.
And it is a vandal's word; it wanders
away from safe places. *And* can be randy, hence
fecund, and capricious, especially at the end of lines. *And*
yet takes a stand amid a band of standard angels.
And issues its one-word command: Continue!
Thus, *and* is also a sinuous riverine word meandering
through the lands of a thousand landscapes;
and expands the Universe. And *and* is
the grand word embedded in love:
grandmother, husband, my daughter
Alexandra, my son Alexander.

We cannot live without our *ands* at hand.
And is the handiest word in all of poetry.

Dottie Weil

The Collar

My father, James Harvey Coomer, was a good talker, and yet we have very little of his story. As for artifacts pertaining to his family, I have just one photo of his mother and one of his father—and a stained shirt collar with two bullet holes in it. My grandfather, the town marshal of Burnside, Kentucky, was wearing the collar the day of August 13, 1913, when he was shot by a man who arrived in town, drunk, on the train from Somerset. The marshal intended to take him to jail to sober up. During the melee, the shooter, Josh Tarter, killed a member of the posse, John Fitzgerald. Marshal Coomer lived nineteen days until he succumbed to the bullet that went through his neck. My father's sister Edna first told me this story when my brother and I were kids, and we, along with our mother, made our one and only visit together to Burnside.

Daddy's references to his boyhood in the hill town of Burnside were brief, typical parental stories about how rough his childhood was compared to our pampered existence. As Jim and I were coping with the challenges of growing up and the many moves of the family due to the Great Depression of the 1930s (I was born on October 29, 1929), we didn't listen attentively or ask, later, for less typical stories. Family dissention, divorce, our adult careers, and our own families crowded out probing into our father's past, which, too late I realized, was an interesting and unusual one, perhaps influencing our own lives in ways we will now never know. Whatever effect the killing had on James Harvey (the middle boy and third eldest of the marshal's eight children) was buried with him.

While we lived together sporadically as a family (as Mother and we children occasionally lived with her family), we knew our father, who was a one-time steamboat captain and mate, patent-medicine promoter, Penny-Saver Bread salesman, marina caretaker, and successful businessman, to also be domineering, funny, restless, hard-working, angry, outgoing but private. He was a ladies' man and a prodigious cusser (for those days), with a steamboat mate's loud voice.

We knew he admired his father, following him onto the steamboats that loaded and unloaded at Burnside when he was a kid. He was proudest of his river career.

The story of his father's death was told to us by Edna, the only one of the siblings who remained in Burnside her whole life. Joe, the youngest brother, I learned, was nostalgic for the home place, and visited, but James Harvey never went back until he was divorced from our mother, and had retired there. The eldest son, Stafford, so far as I know, moved away and never returned. We children never met either of our father's brothers, and we never heard of the men contacting one another after James and Joe served together on the *Americana,* a steamboat that was lost in a fire.

So, we don't know the stories of our uncles' ties to the old hometown, nor our father's. Too late, I thought about the marshal's death and how it might influence his children, especially the boys. One account—on a scrap of newsprint I have saved (source unknown)—says the marshal foreswore any charges against his shooter's family for fear it would provoke his sons into dangerous conflict with the Tarter family. The family of the Mr. Fitzgerald who was killed did press charges and the shooter served time in the penitentiary.

The loss of this grandparent inspired my curiosity and wonderment about its effect over time. I published a semi-fictional story about the incident, along with a poem, and a sketch in my 2002 memoir. My father read the short story and hated it, for I presented Burnside as the dusty little Depression town—the only Burnside I remembered, from one visit as a child—and he recalled the town when he was young as a bustling shipping center for steamboats on the Cumberland River, a place with a sawmill, stores, and a hotel. Of course, now the old town is under the waters of Lake Cumberland, and much of its past buried.

We do know, from contemporary accounts about the death of Marshal John Coomer, that my grandfather was unarmed, having given up carrying a gun after killing a man during an arrest.

I hated the shooter for depriving me of knowing my grandfather, though eventually realizing that we would be unlikely ever to have met. Marshal Coomer would have been sixty-eight when I was born, and the typical age of death at the time was much younger. But I always wanted to know him—I love the photo of him that sits on the table next to my bed—a tall, cocky-looking man in a black suit, hat tipped at a rakish angle, wearing his silver marshal's badge.

My one other memento is the collar Marshal Coomer was wearing when he was shot. It is rusty and stained, with two ragged holes in it. I am not the logical owner of this relic, but it obviously haunted my imagination. Late in life, visiting my Aunt Edna in Burnside, I asked to see it again. And asked if I could have it. She readily agreed and wrapped it in wax paper for me. When asked by several relatives whatever happened to the collar, I did not say anything. I did not want to give it up. It is safe under glass, but I worry about what will happen to it when I am no longer around to take care of it.

I will never know how the violent death of our forebear affected the many generations of my family. My father revered his father, comparing him to a movie version of a town marshal. My father never owned a gun, nor have any of the men in my immediate family.

Beneath my father's complex personality was a kind of pilot light of anger, and I would think his father's unfair death surely was one element that kept it going, though he often joked about the amount of violence in Pulaski County, Kentucky. I feel I might have gotten a bit of that blue flame.

In December of 2006, a monument to the firefighters and marshals killed in Pulaski County in the line of duty was erected in the Law Enforcement and Firefighters Memorial Park near Somerset, Kentucky. Twelve marshals were named, including, of course, my grandfather.

My two sons drove me down to see the monument after it was completed. They are proud of the collar, and of having an illustrious ancestor with a fascinating story, but they do not feel the personal loss I do.

My cousin Jim Ed Fitzgerald followed our grandfather's path in law enforcement and served as a Kentucky State Trooper. He and I have traded information about the marshal—by mail between his home in Harrodsburg, Kentucky, and mine in Cincinnati. For years we vowed to get together—a meeting that never happened, as Jim Ed died this year.

Time, like the waters of the Cumberland River diverted to create Lake Cumberland, covering the old town of my grandfather and his sons and daughters, may have muted the angers and losses of the past. Still, I feel that no one should forget the pain of violent death. I think of Robert Frost's lines, "Blood has been harder to dam back than water / Just when we think we have it impounded safe / Behind new barrier walls (and let it chafe!), / It breaks away in some new kind of slaughter."

KARL PLANK
Grave Stones

In memory of Nelle Clayton Boyette

In a year of shuddering
I tell myself:

Study the rock from which you came
the stones that rise
from the ground

in the churchyard at Sharon
the double-arched marker of twin daughters
who survived 3 days and 6 days in 1852—

The first grave in this cemetery—

and to its right the remains of a child
who lived
one month in the spring of 1862.

Here lie the bones of the twins' father
who took his life in 1866—
Gone to rest, his monument says—

and of the mother who worked
without rest until 1909.
Give her of the fruit of her hands

her children chiseled in rock
to record her resolve, remembering
her left arm

was stump-ended from birth.
The fruit of her hand
it might have read.

When young, Aunt Nelle
would go to Eliza's corner
at the right of the fireplace

to watch her grandmother
sew petticoats with lace borders,
the cloth clasped by a *little bird*

*that worked like a spring clothespin
fastened on the candle stand.*
She pinned the other end to her dress

and brought *the little arm under
like quilting.* The little arm, *it was strong,*
she noted

in a letter to my mother
confessing *I could tell you more clearly
than I can write it.*

And now, over the chasm of years,
I reply
to tell myself:

these words
penned on paper
bring back the lost

or carved in rock
mark what was
and what is not.

They stitch
the vanishing trace
with golden thread.

It might be enough
to hold
the living

the living, that is,
in the hand
of the dead.

Denise Roberts McKinney
The White Pine Cathedral

The woods seduce the word-weaver in me
and I am born again, breathless and giddy.
Child and crone, all at once, indistinguishable
… and it is good!

My very body a holy and living sacrifice—
Temple to Spirit.
Pause. Pray. Rest. Play.
This is my body, given for the sheer joy in giving.

Receive now the blessing of consecration,
for we are indeed keepers and kept.
Creator whispers benediction through the trees
as buzzards answer in flight.

My God! My God!
What have I done to deserve this?
All the joy I can stand, wrapped in each moment,
orgasmic in impact, humbling in the receiving.

Blessed am I among women!
I do not want, for ecstasy fills the soul-shaped need in my bosom
while I reside in the surety that
I know nothing and *it is well with my soul.*

To be at home in the body is to be present with the Holy.
Our dwelling place, abiding,
love shining through all the imperfections,
reminding that nothing is irretrievably broken,

but all the more lovely in the wearing
of this flesh and bone—knit together,
fearfully and wonderfully made,
abundant in sensuality and sacredness,

overflowing from the heart's cup of life
inflowing from stardust and galaxies
from where we came
and where we will tarry.

Roberta Schultz
Bones in the Woods

Lately, all the bones show.
Like a dog who won't let go,

they gnaw at me. Sockets haunt the mirror
where eyes should steal focus. I notice how

my pup's tiny rib niggles at my flesh.
Her jaw unhinges as she sleeps

near my knee. It is time to build
stronger femurs, beg harder mandibles.

Poets like Maggie Smith explore
real estate's "good bones" myth.

She bubbles and brews new healing
broth from sad disaster's plaster cracks.

I cease my need to pick these tibias
strewn across the trail. The baby buck

born in tall grass becomes that skull
cradled in the crook of a granny

grapevine's ulna. I kneel before pelvises
that line this pilgrim path, pass each

roadside shrine to sacred vertebrae.
All scapula and metatarsal chimes

must jangle free, powder dust designs.
Shine through sand and shadow.

Timothy Dodd

Shenandoah

Winter trees, dead trees thousands
and a dusk falling onto rolling hills.

The light slips, cattle in silhouette,
lost tributaries wind their thin way

through the dry tobacco cull, fields
forgotten of Civil War's battle heat.

Barns empty now, bridges whittled
to solitary bases crumbling in shallow.

Mailboxes at the end of gravel lanes,
what have they received? A crooked

roadside sign the rear lights of vehicle
never read, red on bloody modernity.

December snow has forgotten us,
and a moon at its faintest wants not

to impose upon scene. I am out there
somewhere, too, crawling under sky,

searching for the dialect, seeking on
where the gone dead might return us.

Beth Copeland

Trick or Treat, 1957

You come back to haunt me in a white sheet
with eye holes cut too far apart.

Caramels, candy corn, and chocolate kisses
rain into a brown paper bag crayoned with bats,

crescent moons, and hissing cats. Running through the dark,
you cry, *Wait, wait for me! I can't see, I can't see!*

You were the child who passed through seasons
unseen, a blur of light in family photographs,

the one who wasn't allowed to stay up late watching
The Twilight Zone on TV because you were scared

of everything—strangers, ladders, and sidewalk cracks,
afraid to look in the mirror, afraid of what you'd see

or wouldn't see on its breath-fogged surface, afraid
of dying and becoming what you pretended to be.

Chuck Billingsley

Gatlinburg, Tennessee #1

Digital Photography

Ron Houchin

Underworld

The community below the cemetery, fixed
as fish in a frozen river, giving off
bubbles of bacteria and breathless dust,
fit in their boxes as feet into shoes,
time taking long corrosive
steps across them.

When they dropped their biggest wet bag
of grief, left it lying in an alley,
on the living room floor, in a cranked up
hospital bed, or where it exploded
and vaporized in war, they had just
begun to disseminate.

There is almost one down there for every
one living up here. Not vampires hiding,
licking dry fangs and waiting under grass
like ticks, but the recently and long ago
interred whose metaphors must sprout
again and again in us.

Ron Houchin

The Longevity of Smoke Rings

They are born roiling and vigorous,
changing and staying the same
their whole lifespan. Good Buddhists.
Like odorless incense they render
atmosphere in jail cell or celestial hall.
Once broken, they form every cursive
letter of the alphabet. Once gone,
memory lingers, a gong soundless as air.
There's ordinary smoke and there's that
shaped by lips, a language that comes and goes.

Pauletta Hansel, Marc Harshman, & Jim Minick
Remembering Ron Houchin, 1947-2022

Pauletta Hansel:

I am trying to remember when I first met Ron Houchin. Hindman? An early Appalachian Poetry Project reading? Did he just show up with Eddy Pendarvis and Laura Bentley at an 80s SAWC gathering? I think his name and get a whiff of pipe smoke. He looked to be a tougher man than his friends knew him to be. I got to know Ron best during an Appalachian Writers Workshop session with Rebecca Gayle Howell on documentary poetry. Each poet told a story about his or her mother for another poet in the session to write about, and though I was not paired with Ron, I was so taken with his story that I reached out to him and his poetry partner, Leah Cheak, to ask to draft a poem from what they did. Here's a section, eventually published in *Still: The Journal*, written in Ron's voice. I think of it as a sort of origin story of the poet and friend we love and miss:

> I could break into anything—houses, cars.
> We called it joyriding: drive until you
> run it out of gas, leave it empty
> where it lands. I broke my ribs,
> my shoulder, fingers, toes. I broke
> my leg three times—same leg. That last
> fall from somebody else's fire escape
> is what wholly broke me. I landed
>
> in a world of books. What else
> was there to do but read and think,
> those weeks in traction? I always wonder,
> how was it that she knew—

surely she knew?—you have to break
a thing to make a new thing from it.

From "To Break a Thing," *Still: The Journal.* Winter 2018.

Marc Harshman:

Ron and I met many, many years ago in the early days of the James Wright Poetry Festival, let's say the early 1980s. The festival was held across the river from Wheeling in Martins Ferry, Ohio. I remember thinking then that I wished Ron lived closer, that we would have lots to talk about in the world of poetry. Well, he never moved closer, but through miracles of serendipity and coincidence our paths would continue to happily cross. And better yet I would soon come to know and be inspired by his inimitable poetry.

I remember, as well, introducing him a few years ago at the Wheeling Poetry Series where he read along with his close friend, Art Stringer. I said at that time that I could point to many poems exemplifying Ron's diverse talent, but how I thought the following perfect little paragraph from a prose poem, "In My Town: West Virginia," went a long way towards capturing the spirit of Ron's work:

> "There's a cluster of box houses, two streetlights,
> a one-room post office, and a stop sign that circle like wagons against the outside world, each familiar as the items of a bedside table in the kumbayah of
> self-protection."

Many of us know this town, have lived in it, and must tip our hats to its accuracy.

A section of what Ron had to say in a blurb for my book, *Believe What You Can*, read that I spoke to "what can be believed." Well, that was very kind but Ron, as a truly exemplary poet, spoke to what can be believed *beyond belief* and that, that is marvelous, something few ever accomplish.

I'd like to think now…to paraphrase lines from another of Ron's poems, "Young Mare," that, like that mare, Ron has gone "… somewhere into / the night, [to] learn to be heavy while being light." May it be so for him, may it be so for us when our time comes. Ron was a superb poet, as fine as I've known anywhere, any time, and a truly decent human being. His like we may never see again.

In My Town: West Virginia

There's a cluster of box houses, two streetlights, a one-room post office, and a stop sign that circle like wagons against the outside world, each familiar as the items of a bedside table in the kumbayah of self-protection.

Each house has local-color shutters that stutter a chorus in wind, the same small porches that support two pots of geraniums as if an ordinance were passed some years ago against mums; a curious cabbage garden infects each backyard.

Two streetlights work always, except in very high winds; until 2001, we had only one. The R&R track splits the town like a slash through a theta. Each of us as teen spent hours out there with a friend, maybe two, listening to the dying rail hum of distant places.

Our post office has the wood from the pilothouse of a riverboat lodged there so long in water the tiny town accrued around it. If our village's growth were a cancer, the patient would never die.

Mail slots in the post office wear everyone's first name,

except Ricky Morris's and Ricki Lewis's. Their boxes have the |Y and |X signs for last names, the postmaster's acknowledgment that gender similarities exist.

The stop sign at the town limits stands its red watch. The last thing everyone sees before leaving warns to look both ways and watch as the road opens up mountain that's no longer outside our town. It has just begun the eternity of being gone...

From Ron Houchin's *The Man Who Saws Us In Half: Poems.* Louisiana State University, 2013.

Young Mare

She runs, deciding to be sun or wind.
Over the fence, her mane streams
like the cartoon lines for breeze;
she skims the creek, a splash of white.
A thundering, weighted air, she floods fields,
rolling, steady toward some lost gait.
I dream her stopping, sudden as a stump,
to stare at evening where the last meadow
turns to trees, and see her rearing from grass
to kick at stars. She comes late to the window
to watch me sleep, then goes somewhere into
night, learning to be heavy while being light.

Written and shared by Ron Houchin at the Wheeling Poetry Series. Ohio County Public Library. July 17, 2018.

JIM MINICK:

I first met Ron in the late 1990s, either at the Southern Appalachian Writers Cooperative (SAWC) gathering or

Hindman's Appalachian Writers Week, and I admit to being a little intimidated at first by his quiet, steady gaze and reputation. But talking poetry and drinking whiskey joined us.

Then in 2006, our friend Rita Riddle died. She left an unfinished poetry book that needed to be sent out into the world for others to read. SAWC and Iris Press agreed to publish it, and I took on the task of editing. But I was very intimidated by this task—how do you edit someone's work when that someone can no longer say yes or no to your proposed changes, can no longer answer your questions. Ron kindly stepped in, agreeing to help me with the editing. And in his usual quiet, gracious, brilliant way, he taught me much—about lyric and line break, and most importantly, how to listen, or try to listen, to the dead.

Rita's book came out in 2008, and with the proceeds from its sale, we funded a scholarship to send a student to Hindman's annual Writers Workshop. Again, I asked Ron to help, this time to judge the entries, which he did with kindness and dependability. We continued this scholarship for several years, Ron helping judge for everyone.

One year, 2013, I was unable to go to Hindman with the scholarship winner, and Ron sent a note saying to tell her to look for him, he wanted to make her feel welcome. In his typical dry humor, he wrote, "Just have her look for the old white-haired guy in the flashy ball cap."

One other gift from Ron was that he wrote a cover quote for one of my poetry books, his words full of his signature compassion and intelligence. But maybe the best honor from that was he wrote a poem based on one of my poems, or as he said: "I'm attaching a poem that one of your poems made me commit." The line that sparked him to write was "a ghost of a ghost,"—what does it mean to be a ghost of a ghost? I'd like to end with this poem that somehow captures what we're all missing now. We have Ron's poetry and our memories of him, and yet….

One Step Removed

> *a ghost of a ghost…*
> —Jim Minick

If ghost is the body one step
removed, like the wavy reflection
of the moon in the river,
the ghost of the ghost's a memory,
and the ghost of recollection,
a dream. Most nights when I go
down to water's edge in dream,
moon's light lies heavy on my shoulders
and my hand shines when I lift it,
so much like your hand on my hand
when we walked here in wet grass.
Somehow the wet is missing in the dream.

From Houchin's *The Man Who Saws Us in Half*. LSU Press, 2013.

Dana Wildsmith

Pandora

All singing is a gift. Silencing
a song stops our breath from travelling
unhindered reach beyond where hands can touch
or need can claim. Think of how we clutch
the hands of the dying as if we
were holding life itself and could keep
it from leaving by tightening our grip.
Let go. Sing. I watched my own mother slip
morning by morning past full waking,
shaking her head, *no,* until, taking
her curled hand in mine to insist her
once more to my bewildering world,
I'd lead her into song. Easing, she heard
her name in every note and answered,
I remember.

Jennifer Davis Michael
Snakeskin

The snake shedding its skin
looks for two rocks
to squeeze between:
      friction against
      stability
      bringing release.

Myself, age three,
head caught between banisters,
a voice soothing
      my ears, as fingers
      worked the cartilage
      past the cold iron.

After three hours of pushing,
forceps eased my son
through a cradle of bones
      into the shock of air
      and light, the outstretched
      hands of welcome.

My father's skin: a crust
he's starting to slough off.
I kiss his forehead.
      He grasps my hand,
      eyes focused on
      the narrow passage.

Jay Pettit
[I approached the river]

I approached the river,
      or
was it just a small stream?

Either way, an insurmountable
border
      between self and other.

Yet, constantly flowing, continually
      changing, not the same in
two consecutive moments.

And so it goes
with boundaries between people;
      always changing,
      seldom noticed,
      never the same,

we never, really, know what
      they are;
never understand them
especially in depth;

yet we always keep them in place
      as if to let them dissolve
would somehow make us less.

Sherrie Skipper

Pretend I Have No Religion and Let Me Write This Poem

We are told
we can't take money with us.

But I believe we can take grudges
stored up in ourselves
in overhead baggage.

Hates
judgments

stored up in our souls
to work out.

We clinch our fists
and shake them at folks.

The funk in our fists may get stored away.

Who says we are liberated when we die?
If we are mad at God
neighbor
      wife
life

and it's stuck in the grout lines
of our bones
maybe that travels with us to chew on the next time.

Bonnie Proudfoot
Look Away

Instead, count pairs of doves on the porch railing,
crows shouting from the garden fence, alarms
and reminders that chime, the voice of google assistant
insistent and bland. None of those seem too
important, just the clatter of the house,
another way the world intrudes. On the news
more refugees, bombs from Russia burn
and shatter, all things can perish at the whim
of Putin, it seems, as he tells his people
that they are protecting the world. Whose
world, we ask, each of us visualizing
some horror that the world could inflict on
our loved ones, knowing that our homes are made
of wood that burns, stones that crumble.
My mother's friend walked across the Alps,
her entire family lost in Nazi camps, somehow
she walked on. Nothing at the beginning
of her journey, nothing at the end, just her one
precious life. In Guernica, Picasso painted babies
dying, mothers weeping, life shattered, black and white
captured the horror, no mistaking color as joy. Why
do I want to say shock and awe? Someone covered
that tapestry in blue cloth when Powell spoke to the UN.
Again, CNN shows us the aftermath, flattened theatres
filled with children, or hollowed out homes and hospitals,
pregnant women shuttled on stretchers, blood-spattered,
each life dangles in the balance. I have turned off the tv
and turned it on too many times to count, the commercials
all seem to write new words to jingles I've heard before.

GARY PHILLIPS

Weather-Bound

You need to understand: I grew up at the knife-edge end of
 subsistence culture
North Carolina, 1960s, strung between the Cherokee foothills
 and Pisgah

My father prayed for white bread and sturdy shoes when he
 was a child
A boy who sometimes walked barefoot 14 hours a day behind
 a mule's ass.

We followed old ways of foraging, employed beagle hounds,
 gigs, tackle and shotgun
Between chores and pleasures the outside was inside our thin
 house; I love weather

In all its forms, from sheeting rain come down the holler in a
 wave
to a blanket of snow—I greet the weather like a companion,
 speak to it in tones

And prayers, bond my spiritual and emotional life to it-hard
 rain, desert sere
thunder and lightning above rough seas, bitter cold under a
 quilt of stars

gave away my guns when I was in my twenties and joined the
 peace movement
Turned away from that hardscrabble but satisfying life, like a
 perfect academic wife

Inside and tamed, hired and named, currying favors and
 closing my windows at night

Til ten years on and in full flight I landed in Wales, on a 600-
 acre sheep farm by the sea
And on a rainy day that distilled me, with borrowed wellies
 and a hat

I was set out with some companions, then the keeper placed
 into my hands
a 19th century Spanish doubled-barrel with silver-inlay that
 felt so *right*

I looked about to see where I was / the rain drilling down
into the soft earth and saying *rise, rise again,* and a bird burst
 from the wood

and up my arms went to the sky and the stock against my
 shoulder fit; I shot
and the bird plummeted, while my heart beat the staccato of a
 waterfall
and the rain fell and fell, where all dispersed but me and gun
 and gamesmen

I stayed the day and helped to put the birds away, hung on
 tender-hooks to cure
for next week's meal. I was made to drink a dram and dry my
 coat and eat a meal.

Then I went out again, to greet the rain.

Dale Marie Prenatt
General Delivery

Dear Grandma's Well House, Store House, Roof-under-rubble,

      Sure hope this finds you. Am sending General Delivery.
Same as I have so many songs to whichever God runs these hollers.

Dropping a line to tell you they arrested the arsonists.
Volunteer firefighters burned you out. Told us we were lucky

Grandma was already dead. Said a previous hit of Firefighter Arson
killed another grandma snoring in her back room.

      When I slept beside you, Well House, you pumped pure water
from the mountain alive as the rhododendrons. Mourned then

and shared my suspicions. Reckon they were true. We own the veins
of coal the companies can't get to. We own the minerals and the gas

bloating up the earth. It's all heirship-owned and none have paid
to clean you away so the homestead remains an eyesore and target.

I'll wind this up. I do think of you, Well House, Store House, Third Roof
Grandma Bought after the strip mine blasts shook loose the other two.

      I hope this finds what's left of you. A rubble pile monument
under a bald empty mountain ugly and obvious as a felony.

Matt Prater

For Voyager, Leaving the Solar System

Owed to Nikki Giovanni

One needs the urge to go and the urge to stay,
a perfect balance of those two, and a taste for silence.
One needs a stoic intimacy with the long success
that seems like failure for a lifetime, then marks
that life in the memory of all its scoffers' children.
One needs to know about finding and being found.
One needs to know about mistaking, being mistaken,
and all the dangers on each side of that wobbling coin.
One needs to know what not to touch, and how to step
in a river where they haven't stepped before. A genius
for numbers and plasmas would be nice, of course.
But far better to know how to die before we die,
and the difference between that death and the death
of the body or soul. One needs what won't be taught
by Caltech or the branch academies. That being this:
we will find what we bring with us. We always have.
Every monster we've ever imagined was our own projection.
What the conquistadors imagined they saw is what they did.

Byron Hoot

Meandering in Sanctuary

It is Sunday and I do not worry
about running into God today.
I will not run should God come
running after me. I do not check
the hillside nor the horizon. I
am content to meander in the sacredness
of time and place where here
and now is sanctuary and eternity,
the spirit on every breath I breathe.
The pursuit of God is like looking
for your face in a reflection—what
is there is simply there.
To breathe in the rarified air of
reality is communion whereby
neither flesh or blood is consumed,
bread and wine holy enough for
what I need. When I have followed
myself, like I'm on a trail of a deer,
the mysteries have been given to me:
the immaculate, exile and return,
lessons learned, betrayal, judgment,
the sentence of death, the gift of rising
from the dead. Should God come,
depending on the time of day, I'll
offer coffee or beer, a place to sit,
and time—like eternity—to talk for a little bit.

BOOK REVIEWS & NEWS

BOOK REVIEW by THOMAS CROWE

Steve Abhaya Brooks
Joy Amongst the Catastrophe: The Pandemic, Politics, and Climate Change
(Amazon Kindle Editions, 2021) 200 pages; $15, E-Book

Steve Brooks' *Joy Among the Catastrophe*, written during the pandemic lockdown took me by surprise in its departure in style from earlier works of his and in its insights into the effects of catastrophe. In his short introduction to the book, he describes his vision and experience of writing the prose poems that make up this volume. Noting that he began the book just before the stay-at-home order, he says he came to realize that writing "under the threat of death and disease, a climate emergency, systemic racism, and the threat of autocracy in the world's oldest democracy" inspired poems able to "reveal the source of joy that is ever present, even in troubling times."

Entering this doorway into the remarkable room that is this collection, we possibly see Steve Brooks at his all-time best. He has been writing a kind of Eastern poetry he calls Zenku (a term he coined) that pretty much follows all the form rules of the haiku tradition. But in *Joy Among the Catastrophe*, he breaks free from those stylistic rules and writes poems in short paragraphs that are more expansive, and sing. Not only are these poems reminiscent of poets such as Ryokan, Issa, Basho, Wang Wei and Han-Shan, but of Taoist master Lao Tsu, and of a 21st century contemporary, French philosopher-scientist and Buddhist monk, Matthieu Ricard, author of *Happiness*. In short, Brooks' book is a volume of present-day wisdom from someone who has put in time and effort over the course of a lifetime and has "opened the doors of his own perception" as

Huxley would say, and is showing us how to both gain a higher perspective on life on planet Earth amongst all its brands and breeds of humans and how to act and interact with oneself and others within a contemporary framework that we all, during a period of climate change and a pandemic, can relate to. This, then, as an example: "Tiny bundles, like pine cones, bristly pods beneath a tree on the path, each pod, a future tree, no fertile ground to be found, they become work for birds. Resting becomes capture, then flight, then release, then the unknown. I am unseen, until I'm seen, and even then I don't know my fate."

Perhaps my favorite poem from Brooks' new book comes right out of the gate in a poem titled *"Waiting For Love"* that to my mind is the signature poem in the collection. Beginning with an observation, "Waiting for love to surface, knowing it lies beneath this exquisite pause. Looking for love beyond oneself depends on its origin within," the prose poem ends, "I'm swamped by love, my boat goes under, until I become its craft. If you see me, do not save me, I am found in the awakening dream. Alive in its peace, I come out of love into love's expression."

In a more physical/political vein are poems such as the poem entitled *"Years From Now."* This short poem and others recognize and honor our vulnerability and the strength in our connectedness.

You get the picture. Or do you? To get the full picture of the nature of true nature and what might be called "higher love," read *Joy Among the Catastrophe*. The collection has much original insight to share. That said, and in summing up, let me share one final poem that serves as a kind of exclamation point at the end of a remarkable and must-read book. "If cherry trees can blossom during this dark spring, why can't we, as well? Those out running, walking, those in their yards, blossom with smiles, good words. Good nature takes root, along with the bad, flowers accompany weeds, apple shelters in place, magnolia stays at home, showing their colors. If cherry trees can blossom during this dark spring, may we be as bright."

An expanded version of this review appeared in the December 15, 2021, edition of *Smoky Mountain News*.

BOOK REVIEW by TIMOTHY DODD

Jacob Strautmann
The Land of the Dead is Open for Business
(New York, NY, Four Way Books, 2020) 80 pages; $16.95, paper

Hailing from the town of Cameron in West Virginia's northern panhandle, Jacob Strautmann has written an excellent collection of poetry firmly grounded in the traditional themes and concerns of his birthplace. It is the poet's language and rich imagery, however, that asserts and carves out a space of its own, pouring lexiconic gravy over the territory of our Appalachian staples. While *The Land of the Dead is Open for Business* is rooted decisively in the author's cultural heritage, Strautmann weaves his own original and connective quilt with wording that is at times both accessible and arcane, yet over reliant on neither. Confident in its originality and distinctive march, this is a creatively crafted poetry casting clear pictures in our minds, poignantly delivering both the values and true-to-life sense of place that is West Virginia.

Despite the forlorn quality of the sepia cover and select poems which do indeed reiterate the collection's ironically tragic title, all is not catastrophe and sadness here. Far from it. In fact, life is brimming in these pages, and titles such as "Mayor Betty's Cameron Crawdad Fest" and "Ramp Hunting" are enough to prove it. From nostalgic to lamenting and racked to praised, the steady beat of life is on offer here, poems diverse yet consistent and faithful to the pulse and pleasures, ills and wills of small town and rural West Virginia living. While poems such as "Buffalo Creek" and "The Assumption" effectively ride on the hurt that modernization and commerce drive onto the land, it is ultimately the cultural and personal experiences, traditional life, that is the heart of the collection. But like any good and knowledgeable Appalachian, Strautmann's voice ultimately cedes all our human endeavors, positive or negative, to the power and destiny of the land, and whether in elegy or regret—often a mixture of both—these poems are sure to sound the siren of life's fragility and passing.

Numerous examples could be pointed out as fine evidence, but the final stanza of a poem found early in the collection, "What's Left," is particularly indicative of Strautmann's power and drive:

> a turn, there was nothing to forgive,
> precambrian death magnificently still
> but for the moon, that living pockmark,
> stitching it all back, pulling bare the threaded night.
> The curtain shook, the wind rising.
> When I said *parent*, I meant topography.

The themes and stylistics noted above fit together even more tightly in his "Mercy Prayer," a revealing title in which life and land pleads for grace. This poem begins with the land personified, yearning:

> The hills tire of propping
> what's left, dream to be
> a tract-less plain
> combed by the wind,

From there, the poem flows directly into images and themes of the lives of inhabitants: small town concerns, big-city do or don't, relationships—yet all still remains strongly but subtly tied to the hills that began the poem:

> long like bored boys
> in Cameron High's Vo-Ag
> for a gun, a treestand,
> last night's girl scent

> lingering. They cup
> their hands. stay warm,
> breathe deeply, know
> the cost of staying
> the cost of Pittsburgh
> is no alternative.

The poem continues to propel forward on these themes, tightly, impacting, before ending on a prayer and the powers beyond human endeavor, potency. All of it, again, emits a strong projection of Appalachian identity, life, love, challenge, and concern—soul, if you will: the propensity to hope despite our own strong fatalism and recognition of weakness.

> Spin us—oh World—
> spin us a second time,
> out Grapevine, out Saltlick,
> wield us light.

This, then, is the essence of an excellent collection of poetry: a poetry of Appalachian doubt, faith, pillars, cries, urgings—a reflection of our region's vibrancy and tragedy, life itself. Coming together sweetly in Jacob Strautmann's fine craftwork, the spirit of Appalachian song carries through the hills.

BOOK REVIEW by DONNA MEREDITH

Michael Henson
Secure the Shadow

(Athens, Ohio University Press, 2021) 255 pages; $22.95, paper

A series of photographs ties the various characters together in Michael Henson's literary novel *Secure the Shadow*. Amy Taylor is a middle-class teen who becomes intrigued by the inner-city people she passes as she walks to her art school. They include professional photographer Paul Lewis, an alcoholic named Jenny, a Black child named Jonathan, and Daniel, a young drug dealer. Amy's exposure to them widens her constricted worldview.

Henson skillfully creates images to illustrate how his characters embody the novel's themes of fear, rage, and power. For example, Jenny's mother "seethed with an incredible wounding and anger that were constantly rising in her like yeast and that constantly filled the kitchen with an odor of bread and iron." Jenny herself lives with a fear that "entered her like a virus." It "was a coat thrown across her shoulders. It was a screen down before her eyes." The photographer Paul had "rolled out to California at nineteen on a wave of loneliness and rage. . . . so bearish and so unrelated to any identifiable or blamable thing in his life . . . that he had trouble recognizing it as his own. But by the age of nineteen it had become his road partner, his companion, and was not to be left at home nor buried along the way without violating some sort of code of loyalty and right." And then there's Amy, whose voice carries many of the chapters. Like most daughters, she wants power over her mother:

She wanted to know what her father's power

was made of. And a desire came up in her,
sudden and irrational and wholly without
precedent or history: she wanted a power like
that. She wanted to be able to put that quaver
in her mother's voice.

But her father was untouchably and
perpetually on the road, sharing his power
with strangers. . . . So for a long time her
desire for a power like that disappeared. It
crawled up into the cliffs and slept like a bear.

Eventually, Amy finds power by rebelling against her mother's restrictions. Amy admires the way Paul's photography captures the humanity of marginalized people, and she is determined to study with him despite her mother's vague dismissal of her newfound interest. Forging her mother's signature on a school permission slip, Amy begins an internship with Paul. Detailed descriptions of their photos are frequently employed as sections of the novel.

The dialogue, especially that of the boy, Jonathan, is particularly well written. Jonathan bridges the worlds of the middle class and street people, chatting freely with both and making a rather likeable pest of himself. He skips school and follows Daniel around, watching drug transactions. The author presents Daniel as a fully complex human, protective of Jonathan and Amy, even as the crack he sells causes harm to many others. Although at first Jonathan seems like an incidental character, his actions have far-reaching consequences for everyone in his orbit.

All the characters here share the need to see and be seen, the need for recognition and power. Inevitably, the strong conflicting emotions boil over into tragedy. Read *Secure the Shadow* for the beautiful language, the poetry of

Henson's prose—and read it to ponder what it says about our world when people across the social spectrum are filled with such fear and rage and loneliness.

BOOK REVIEW by PHILIP ST. CLAIR

Marianne Worthington
The Girl Singer
(Lexington, University Press of Kentucky, 2021)
104 pages; $29.95, hardcover; $19.95, paper

Marianne Worthington's first book of poetry, *Larger Bodies Than Mine* (Finishing Line Press, 2006), earned her the Appalachian Book of the Year Award in 2007. Its hallmarks—crisp language, unforgettable images, emotional depth—are once again prominent in her latest book, *The Girl Singer* (University Press of Kentucky, 2021), recipient of this year's Weatherford Award for poetry.

"Rank Stranger," the first poem, is set apart by way of prologue. Its title is taken from a gospel classic and bluegrass standard by Alfred Brumley. It tells the story of someone raised up in the mountains returning home after a long absence, unable to find kinfolk and friends:"Everybody I met / seemed to be a rank stranger . . ." We see the poet drive west on a dark, rain swept highway in an urbanized, industrialized Appalachia on the banks of the Ohio River: the oil refineries of Ashland, Kentucky loom in the distance. She broods over the words of a poet "who claimed / her grandmother lived such old ways / it was as if all time had stopped, / like she had jammed *her thorn broom / handle into the world's axis.*" Her reaction to this extravagant trope is to refute it: "Still, / The Ohio River curls on as I hit / the highway toward home." Like the irresistible flow of a great river and the inevitable passage of time, Appalachia cannot be confined to rigid, idealized mindsets, and the poems in Worthington's book illustrate this with style, grace, humor, and wisdom.

The product of a bygone era, the term "girl singer" is both demeaning and dismissive: the female vocalist becomes an objectified appendage to a dance band or a traveling show. (In 1935 the sublime Ella Fitzgerald was almost turned down for her first real singing job because bandleader Chick Webb thought her "gawky and unkempt.") We see the girl singer, hungry for fame, as she begins her musical career in the male-dominated radio road shows that played in school halls and county fairs: she is forced into a cultural stereotype that tells corny hillbilly jokes and wears sunbonnets and calico dresses. Growing up, she loved to sing the traditional ballads and "murder songs," but these proved to be too downbeat and old-fashioned for her bosses: "How hard / it was to fetch my voice for chirpier songs." Worthington also showcases women of country music who had broken free of such restrictive roles and became successful and influential on their own terms: Mother Maybelle and Sara Carter, Patsy Cline, Loretta Lynn, Dolly Parton, and most notably Hazel Dickens—singer / songwriter, bluegrass pioneer, labor activist.

Larger Bodies is almost entirely devoted to family history, and it's a pleasant surprise that some of the poems in *Girl Singer* share the same subject. We hear a grandmother who "had a hitch and quaver / in her chatter like a flickering light" ("Vocal School"). We see the relics left by the father who has recently passed away: "… starched pajamas folded / to rest, the wheelchairs / and walkers, the cornucopia of plastic urinals.…" ("Thanksgiving Eve"). We see folks from her mother's side of the family making gestures as they talk, their arms "hefty punctuations signaling a punchline" and "their hands / … veined arrows, always pointing the right way" ("My Maternal People").

In Worthington's Appalachian bestiary, birds reign

supreme. In "Roll Call," the poet invests eight different birds with tarot-card significance: Goldfinch the Acrobat, Mourning Dove the Saint, and so on. Crow, a recurring image throughout the collection, is given his traditional role of the Trickster: Love Crow Daddy perches on the poet's roof, indifferent to the clamor of hostile birds below him as he sets the stage for a Snopes-style invasion of his kin. Once again she becomes preoccupied with the criticism of a poet "who warned / me of my *disingenuous tendency* to give human / qualities to the animals in my poems." She imagines Crow Daddy's response— brief, coarse, appropriate. And in "Put Upon By Grief," a bird becomes both comforter and messenger when a woman "in her worst sorrow" prays for a sign from her departed husband "and a velvet wisp of wing floated / right down to her lap."

One of the joys in *Girl Singer* is its homage to country music. "I Saw Bobby Bare Kiss Marty Stuart," the most ambitious piece in the collection, is centered on the poet's visit to Nashville's Ryman Theater. Consisting of 42 couplets running over four pages, its form serves as an excellent vehicle for a breathless, headlong appreciation of an experience that prompts her to slip in and out of her past. She recalls that her parents had stopped at the Ryman sixty years earlier on their honeymoon, and when the Grand Ole Opry Square Dancers come out to clog, she becomes homesick as she remembers the televised music shows her parents would watch on Saturday afternoons. She recalls the first time she saw fifteen-year-old Marty Stuart play mandolin with Lester Flatt's band "and I fell dead in love with him / that very moment." Forty years later she takes pride that Marty, now a progressive force in country music, has brought back both the spirit and the format of those old broadcasts: "an opening hit, a comic, a guest / or two, the girl singer, and hymn time . . . "As the poem ends, she stands on the sidewalk outside the theater and listens to the people as they exit. She hears "German and Spanish and maybe Bengali" and realizes that they too "love this exceptionally long musical / that crosses decades and languages . . ."

The Girl Singer is a valuable addition to contemporary Appalachian literature. It is the work of a gifted poet at the top of her form, and she has never sung better.

BOOK REVIEW by A. E. STRINGER

Hilda Downer
When Light Waits for Us

(Charlotte, NC, Main Street Rag, 2021) 67 pages; $14, paper

Despite the popular impression that writing is a solitary pursuit, finding the right words is, more often than not, a collaborative effort, even if the 'author' seems primary. In her recent collection, *When Light Waits for Us*. Hilda Downer acknowledges the many sources that fed these poems. In a short introduction, she sees the working of a writer's imagination as akin to our daily collaborations with subject, place, immediate sensation, memory, and with beloved friends and family.

These poems trace the reaching of a self through time toward that light of clarity that a creative life chases without ever quite catching. The arts help us re-gather the living fibers of what is lost in the passage of time, and grasp experience anew. The sources of the subjects rendered movingly in these poems include her childhood, one of severe deprivation; her closest friends; her deep affection for nature; and one particularly long-standing love affair. That life-altering relationship, which was also a poetic collaboration with the photos of her former partner, is a major thread of the book.

A poem that echoes the prose introduction, "Bowerbirds," vividly describes the early collaboration with her partner: "I would help you out—/ suggest an arch of broom sedge / lit by the stained glass / of bluets and violet petals." The images the poet draws from the photos taken in the woods are particularly apt, as these spring blooms will fade even more quickly than other things we hold dear. The same poem addresses the geographic distance between the partners, one of several impediments to a more immediate and fulfilling relationship: "All we want is to write or take photos / and be together, / but we cannot find the way / when responsibility for the people / and places we love is stronger than want." As usual, what we want is tempered by circumstance.

The book's first section holds a grouping of poems inspired by objects such as tables, buttons, clothespins, lipstick. Objects, like photos, hold the form of their origins and carry our recollections forward. These poems showcase Downer's talent for capturing a thing's immediacy in fine sensory detail while also suggesting human values. One poem considers a towel-curtain in a window and the urge to transcend the daily limitations of subsistence living. Even a "towel hole / holds its own / against the bright sky. / Broken threads and those tightly strung / could yield music that stops all war." One of the finest of these object poems is "Buttons," which meditates almost sensually on the variety of buttons in a jar left behind by a grandmother's passing. The buttons, their rich colors and odd shapes, have been carefully saved for re-use, and even for ornamentation, by a woman who "wore no jewelry." To the speaker they are like memories vividly reborn in the present. Of course, the passage of time itself is another major thread in the book. When the speaker returns the buttons to their jar, it becomes "an hourglass starting over again / with fewer seconds left to use."

As the poet Mark Strand once mused, "Time: that's the only problem." One of his contemporaries, Tess Gallagher, considered poems as time machines, allowing us to inhabit multiple times in the moment of the poem. Downer's free verse lyrics often form themselves around juxtapositions of different times or places, allowing her, as time traveler, to bring together past and present, here and there. While this approach risks a reader's possible confusion, Downer is adept at storytelling. She can create a kind of timelessness in which memory's narratives enlighten the present of both poet and reader.

The book's title phrase *When Light Waits for Us* plays with human understanding of relativity and time. Downer's familiarity with a scientific worldview is apparent in many of the poems. She recognizes the dual nature of light, knows that in fact light never waits, that it moves ever onward, even as the lamp that glows in a window remains stationary and able to illuminate both scene and viewer. To reach, through poetry, for the light that "waits for us" speaks to a faith in the eternal.

In Section Two's "Distant Roads," the initial stanza sets a scene on the speaker's dirt road at home, and stanza two jump-cuts to a sunset out a city window, "your window." This near-simultanaeity links the poet and her distant lover/collaborator. In "Plank House," the speaker sits on the porch of an old friend's abode, remembering his artistry, which leads to an insight about the collaborations of love and art: "I want to write something / so meaningful and good / that it might reach the unborn / . . . breaking barriers of time and cognition / so that I could express this sad longing."

Section Two rounds out with poems about family. "Song for Meade" displays a deft handling of form and repetition to characterize the son's mountain upbringing as well as the speaker's longing for his return: "Friends gather on the porch. / Fog trails gauze through mountain loneliness. / Rock-faced cliffs echo, / when are you coming back, back, back?" Downer's ear for language spices the long poem "Message to the Unborn": "even while cobbler / bubbles purple over a browning crust / or a timber rattler stumbles into the clearing, / unable to discern, / amid thick berries, / a bird from a small hand." The poem is a rich evocation of her sorrow for the fouling of our earthly home, and it is filled with intelligence: "The delicate microcosm of humus, / . . . yield[s] orchids so specialized / their pollination requires / one particular species of insect." We can here appreciate the poet's insight into the subtle relationships that nurture the life of local places across time: "Generations away, / no white trillium / will be allowed to offer its hope / against the charred forest floor."

In the book's final section are poems that stand as tentative fulfillments of the themes developing throughout. There are object meditations like "Utility Poles"; stories of important places recalled, as in "Orchard"; long friendships in "Going Home"; and poetic collaborations with the photographs that begin, and punctuate, the book. The poet's deep immersion in the natural, enunciated in the book's epigraph by Whitman, is reaffirmed here, in the poem "You Can Find Me in the Woods" (echoing the bard's "Look for me under your boot soles"). "Just one highway," Downer writes, "—miles and miles / of animals unsettled and dispersed, open for slaughter— / what would these trees have us speak for them? / Let us find the words." As in "Message to the Unborn," it is poetry speaking with the voice of the earth itself that most resonates.

The book's last poems attempt a coming-to-terms with memories of old friends as well as with the lost lover and through it all, the passage of this speaker's life. In "Gray Fossil Site," "Dirt roads flashed mica / bright enough to sting light green eyes / with wonder and terror of what / 'forever and ever' could mean." Photographs of scenes in which our younger selves appear can document memories and prompt questions about the nature of change: "The field we walked has given itself / over to saplings and briars. . . . Did the beauty of this day not exist / without proof?" It can seem sometimes as if we never existed at all, as the past fades like very old photographs. All we have are those moments of beauty and meaning, many of which are experienced in solitude and through poems. The last collaboration is with oneself. As Downer concludes: "I stand alone in the silky glow, / fine as powder on a moth wing, / that lingers awhile before the cool / night air beckons me / toward the light inside."

NEW BOOKS

Compiled by
EDWINA PENDARVIS

An ongoing feature of *Pine Mountain Sand & Gravel* is an annual listing of recent book titles and publishers' blurbs from past and present contributors.

SUPPORT YOUR REGIONAL AUTHORS!

Ellen Austin-Li's chapbook, *Lockdown: Scenes from Early in the Pandemic,* revisits the COVID-19 pandemic in its first months, the time when fear had to be damped down in the face of a global threat. Her poetry remembers in compelling terms the dire results and varied responses to that world-wide challenge. (Finishing Line Press, 2021)

KB Ballentine's *Edge of the Echo*, through its lyric poetry suggests the combination of intimacy and awe that inspired pagan religions of ancient times and, in a sense, implies that rivers, skies, landscapes, and the life that populates them are the source of our history and the path to our future. (Iris Press, 2021)

Sam Barbee, in *Apertures of Voluptuous Force*, "opens a portal on a world in tumult, storms inside and out" writes Valerie Nieman, who describes his poems as both timely and "a riot in language, images detonating against each other . . . a poetry of paradox and opposition." (Red Hawk Publications, 2022)

Roy Bentley's *Hillbilly Guilt*, latest poetry collection won the Hidden River Arts/Willow Run Poetry Book award in 2019. The work epitomizes celebrated characteristics of Appalachian poetry—natural language, a strong sense of place, and the honoring of working-class life. (Hidden River Publishing, 2021)

Ken Chamblee's *If Not These Things* reflects the mystery and meaning inherent in even the mundane occurrences that make up our lives. Set in the vastness of the universe, such occurrences hint at undreamed of possibility and, at the same time, the sense of doom that sometimes touches even the most pragmatic among us. (Kelsay Books, 2022)

Selfie with Cherry, **Beth Copeland**'s chapbook presents, as the title shows, an ironic, millennial sense of life's pain and pleasure. These "bittersweet" poems juxtapose moments of exuberance with the "sobering sense of loss" that gives joy its color (Glass Lyre, 2022).

Todd Davis' poetry collection, *Coffin Honey*, tells three stories suggesting reasons so many of us, in Appalachia and elsewhere, feel a sense of dread as we end the first quarter of the 21st century still out of sync with each other and the natural world. (Michigan State University, 2022)

The poems in **Victor Depta**'s *Eternity is That* illustrate the human impulse to assign names and meaning to what we encounter despite knowing we can never fully understand the world beyond our vision and our fingertips except, perhaps, through fleeting moments of enlightenment. (Blair Mountain Press, 2021)

Timothy Dodd's collection, *The Modern Ancient*, proposes that knowledge of ancient truths leads to fuller understanding of our own lives. The poems argue convincingly the value of creative expression with its connection to mythic experience. (High Window Press, 2022)

Timothy Dodd and Steve Lambert's *Men in Midnight Bloom* strikes Sheldon Lee Compton as "call and response" fiction.

The first story, by Lambert, is echoed in theme by the second story, written by Dodd, and then, vice versa—a story by Dodd is echoed in a story by Lambert. (Cowboy Jamboree Press, 2022)

Hilda Downer's poetry collection, *When Light Waits for Us*, is reviewed in this issue of *PMS&G*. (Main Street Rag Publishing, 2022)

Wiley's Last Resort, by **Hilda Downer** is a paean to Jim Webb, poet, disc jockey, activist, and organizer of annual "soirees" in Whitesburg, Kentucky. Richard Hague describes the poetry as a "document of large love, devoted craft, and rich memories." The cover art is by "Get-In Jesus" T-shirt illustrator, Robert Gipe. (Redhawk Publishing, 2022)

Sue Weaver Dunlap's second poetry collection, *A Walk to the Spring House*, is compared to Lee Smith's novels by author Darnell Arnoult, who writes that the poems stay close to the southern Appalachian landscape and the influence of history, especially regional and familial history, where "each generation is an embodiment of all that comes before." (Iris Press, 2021)

Nettie Farris's new chapbook, *The Alice Poems* traverses both new and familiar territory. The collection's prose poems are written in the voice of Alice, the timeless Alice of Lewis Carroll's classic wonderland, but an older Alice who lives "nearly entirely in her head," using her wits to cope with the nonsensical world outside. (Dancing Girl Press, 2022)

The Berea Chronicles, by **Chris Green**, is a trilogy of chapbooks of haiku, that form's immediacy recognizing the beauty of the apparently insignificant: *The Deepening* (Summer 2012-Winter 2013); *Black Locust* (Spring, 2014-Fall, 2015); and *Crow's Feet* (Winter 2015-Winter 2017). SAWC members can email Chris at greenchr@merea.edu for a free PDF of the trilogy. (Z⁰A, 2020)

Chris Green's poetry collection, *Lower Hell fer Certain: Poems for Artists Thr!ve*, based on his participation in Artists Thr!ve's 2019 summit, when artists of diverse races, ethnicities, and backgrounds came to Berea and also visited Leslie County in eastern Kentucky. The PDF of *Lower Hell fer Certain* is available free at https://artiststhrive.org/summit/summitpoetry. (Artists Thr!ve, 2019)

Rebecca Griswold's *The Attic Bedroom* poetry collection tells a story about the forces that influence membership in cults. The narrative is described as formally inventive and powerful. The poems tell a story through two a past and present perspective, one showing cult allegiance, the other showing the wisdom of hindsight. (Milk and Cake Press, 2022)

Kari Gunter-Seymour edited the anthology, *I Thought I Heard a Cardinal Sing: Ohio's Appalachian Voices*, a collection of poems which illustrates the diversity of writers with deep connections to Appalachian Ohio, a region that is often regarded as different *from* the outside world, but possessing little diversity within itself. (Sheila-Na-Gig Editions, 2022)

Jeff Hardin's collection, *Watermark*, reflects on the desire to know even what may be unknowable—especially in our current society, in which truth is more and more elusive. Jane Satterfield describes these poems as offering "deliberations and debates" that examine faith and the transcendentalist concept of spirit. (Madville Publishing, 2022)

Marc Harshman refers humorously to his *Two Views of Oxford* as a "chaplet." According to the publisher, the book's fifteen pages consist of two meditative pastoral poems illustrated with engravings that depict the historic university and its environs. (Monongahela Books, 2021)

The publisher's description of **Marc Harshman**'s *Dark Hills of Home* notes that the poetry was born "among the foothills and hollows of the western Alleghenies, between the Ohio and Monongahela rivers in the heart of Appalachia." Harshman himself thinks of this collection as, in part, a celebration of his tenth year as West Virginia's poet laureate. (Monongahela Books 2022)

Melissa Helton's second poetry collection, *Forward Through the Interval*, illustrates what Doug Van Gundy means when he says that among the things he loves best about her work is her versatility, precision, and inventiveness. *Forward Through the Interval* is one of four collections selected for the 2021 Workhouse Writers Chapbook Series. (Workhorse Publishing, 2021)

Michael Henson's novel, *Secure the Shadow*, is reviewed in this issue of *PMS&G*. (Ohio University Press, 2021)

Alexandra McIntosh's poetry collection, *Bowlfuls of Blue*, contemplates the beauty and violence of nature and the experience of the earth's communities, composed by nature, geography, or spiritual ideals. Her poems, set in Kentucky and the Ohio River Valley, remember ancestors, childhood, and time with loved ones. (Assure Press, 2021)

John Mannone's *Flux Lines*, fittingly published on Valentine's Day, in updated spirit of the 17th century metaphysical poets, uses metaphors drawn from the physical sciences to give new meaning to the tumultuous feelings associated with being romantically smitten. (Linner's Wings Press, 2022)

In the Lonely Backwater, by **Valerie Nieman**, tells the story of a seventeen-year-old girl dealing with the murder of her teenage cousin. Beth Castrodale calls Maggie's character complex, her fascination with Linnaeus' classification of species adding dimension in suggesting her need for order and understanding. (Regal House Publishing, 2022)

Roberta Schultz's poetry collection, *Underscore*, inspired in part by the corona virus pandemic, reflects the universal "power of song" and of the "daily rhythms of a meditative life." Pauletta Hansel writes that the poems in this collection offer readers "solace, humor, wisdom, beauty, and an occasional welcome jolt." (Dos Madres Press, 2022)

Glamoury, the last of **Susan Sheppard**'s many poetry collections, was published posthumously. Its poetry is haunting and mysterious, as was the poet herself. Grace Cavalieri writes, "Every page of *Glamoury* is rich, resolving to bring truth to life with language smoldering, ready to burst into flame." (Better World Books, 2021)

Ann Shurgin's poetry collection, *While the Whippoorwill Called*, is described by Linda Parsons as "a sensual delight rooted in laurel thicket and balsam ridge." The poems express and elicit pleasure in and closeness to the natural world as well as in the narrator's progress toward a return home to Appalachia. (Redhawk Publications, 2022)

Allison Thorpe's *Reckless Pilgrims* chronicles the beauty in old things, including difficult as it might be, the beauty in her own aging body. The poems reflect on a back-to-the-land way of life, the loss of her husband, and the reconciliation of past and present furnished by memory's keepsakes as she returns to life in the city. (Broadstone Books, 2021)

Richard Tillinghast's latest poetry collection, *Blue if Only I could Tell You*, won the White Pine Press Poetry Prize in 2021. Joe Wilkins, who judged the entries, describes Tillinghast's collection as "plainspoken, clear-eyed, and wise," featuring journeys to and arrivals in "the many far and consequential places we find ourselves." (White Pine Press, 2022)

Susan O'Dell Underwood's novel, *Genesis Road*, tells the story of Glenna, a 36-year-old "run-away" trying to deal with a miscarriage and a third divorce. In the company of an old friend, Glenna heads west, where she finds a modicum of peace and healing enough to find her way back home. (Madville Publishing, 2022)

Marianne Worthington's *The Girl Singer* is reviewed in this issue of *PMS&G*. (University Press of Kentucky, 2022)

CONTRIBUTORS

Mischelle Anthony's poems lately appear in *Cimarron Review, Little Patuxent Review, Cream City Review, Typehouse, Midwest Quarterly, riverSedge, Ocean State Review,* and in her collection, *[Line]* (Foothills Press). She has also edited an 1807 memoir of sexual assault, *Lucinda; Or, The Mountain Mourner* (Syracuse University Press). She lives and works in Wilkes-Barre, Pennsylvania.

Ellen Austin-Li's poetry has appeared in *Artemis, Thimble Literary Magazine, The Maine Review, Rust +Moth,* & elsewhere. Her chapbooks, *Firefly* (2019) & *Lockdown: Scenes from Early in the Pandemic* (2021) were published by Finishing Line Press. Ellen earned an MFA in Poetry from the Solstice Low-Residency Program. She lives with her husband in a newly-empty nest in Cincinnati, OH.

Victoria Woolf Bailey's poems have appeared in a number of publications including *Still, the Journal, Pegasus, The Heartland Review, and Kudzu,* as well as the Motif 3 anthology *All the Livelong Day* published by MotesBooks. Her first full-length collection *Cannibalism and the Copenhagen Interpretation: a Love Story* was released by Finishing Line Press in March 2022. KB Ballentine's seventh collection, *Edge of the Echo,* was released May 2021 with Iris Press. Her earlier books can be found with Blue Light Press, Middle Creek Publishing, and Celtic Cat Publishing. Published in *Atlanta Review* and *Haight-*

Ashbury Literary Journal, among others, her work also appears in anthologies including *The Strategic Poet* (2021), *Pandemic Evolution* (2021), and *In Plein Air* (2017). Learn more at www.kbballentine.com.

Sam Barbee has a new collection, *Uncommon Book of Prayer* (2021, Main Street Rag). His poems recently appeared in *Poetry South*, *Literary Yard*. His collection, *That Rain We Needed* (2016, Press 53), was nominated for Roanoke-Chowan Award as one of North Carolina's best 2016 poetry collections; a two-time Pushcart nominee.

Gershon Ben-Avraham writes short stories and poetry. His short story, "Yoineh Bodek," (*Image*) received "Special Mention" in the *Pushcart Prize XLlV: Best of the Small Presses 2020 Edition*. Kelsay Books published his chapbook *God's Memory* in 2021. Ben-Avraham holds an MA in Philosophy (Aesthetics) from Temple University.

Jessica Weyer Bentley is an Author/Poet. Her first collection of poetry, *Crimson Sunshine*, was published in May 2020 by AlyBlue Media. She has contributed work to several publications for the Award-Winning Book Series, Grief Diaries, including *Poetry and Prose*, and *Hit by a Drunk Driver*. Jessica's work has been anthologized in *Women Speak Vol. 6* (Sheila-Na-Gig Editions), *Summer Gallery of Shoes* (Highland Park Poetry), *Common Threads 2020 Edition* (Ohio Poetry Association), *Pine Mountain Sand & Gravel: Appalachian Witness* (Volume 24) and *Made and Dream* (Of Rust and Glass, 2021), and online blogs including *Global Poemic* and *Fevers of the Mind*. Jessica currently resides in Northwest Ohio.

Roy Bentley is the author of *Walking with Eve in the Loved City*, chosen by Billy Collins as a finalist for the Miller Williams prize; *Starlight Taxi*, winner of the Blue Lynx Poetry Prize; *The Trouble with a Short Horse in Montana*, chosen by John Gallaher as winner of the White Pine Poetry Prize; as well as *My Mother's Red Ford: New & Selected Poems 1986 – 2020* published by Lost Horse Press. Poems have appeared in *Pine Mountain Sand & Gravel, The Southern Review, Rattle, Shenandoah, New Ohio Review, Prairie Schooner,* and *december*, among others. His latest is *Beautiful Plenty* (Main Street Rag Books, 2021).

Chuck Billingsley is a documentary photographer, writer, and self-taught visual artist. He grew up in the Upper Cumberland region of Tennessee. His photographic work is currently focused on documenting the ever-changing landscape of the American Southeast. Chuck currently lives in the suburbs of Nashville and shares his work through his blog, *The Low Gravy*: www.TheLowGravy.com

Jerry Buchanan is a poet who lives in Johnson City, Tennessee. He writes to express his creative voice and to connect with others. His published poems appear in *Quill & Parchment, the American Diversity Report,* and *Black Moon Magazine*. He honed his poetry writing skills with a small group of Appalachian poets called the Seasoned Writers' Group.

Pam Campbell favors the song-like qualities of poetic form & how form serves to contain human suffering & joy. Her poems have appeared in *Ó Bhéal Five Words Vol XIV & Vol XIV Anthologies, 2021 Lexington Poetry Month Anthology, 2021 Blue Mondays Poetry Anthology, &* her prose in *Pine Mountain Sand & Gravel, Literary Journal, Volume 24: Appalachian Witness*

Kenneth Chamlee is the 2022 Gilbert-Chappell Distinguished Poet for the western region of the North Carolina Poetry Society. His poems have appeared in *The North Carolina Literary Review, Tar River Poetry, Blue Mountain Review*, and many others, including seven editions of *Kakalak: An Anthology of Carolina Poets*. His new book of poems, *If Not These Things,* is forthcoming from Kelsay Books in 2022.

Carson Colenbaugh is an undergraduate student of forestry and horticulture at Clemson University, where he researches the environmental history of the southern Appalachians. His poems have appeared or are forthcoming in *Chautauqua, Delta Poetry Review, Pine Mountain Sand and Gravel, Poetry South*, and elsewhere.

Beth Copeland is the author of *Blue Honey,* recipient of the 2017 Dogfish Head Poetry Prize; *Transcendental Telemarketer* (Blaze VOX 2012); and *Traveling through Glass,* recipient of the 1999 Bright Hill Press Poetry Book Award. Her chapbook *Selfie with Cherry* is forthcoming from Glass Lyre Press. She owns Tiny Cabin, Big Ideas™, a writer's retreat in the Blue Ridge.

Thomas Rain Crowe is an internationally published author of more than thirty books, including the multi-award winning nonfiction nature memoir *Zoro's Field: My Life in the Appalachian Woods;* collections of poetry including a volume of love poems titled *Learning To Dance; The Laugharne Poems*--written at the Dylan Thomas boathouse in Laugharne, Wales and published by Carreg Gwalsh in Wales; and a memoir, *Starting From San Francisco: Beats, Baby Beats and the 1970s San Francisco Renaissance*. He is translator of the poetry of Sufi mystic poet Hafiz (*In Wineseller's Street,* Ibex/IranBooks and *Drunk on the Wine of the Beloved,* Shambhala). Founder of New Native Press, Crowe has spoken widely on the subject of higher consciousness, sustainability and protection of the planet. Crowe lives in the Tuckasegee watershed and the "Little Canada" community of Jackson County in western North Carolina.

Todd Davis is the author of seven full-length collections of poetry, most recently *Coffin Honey* and *Native Species,* both published by Michigan State University Press. He has won the Midwest Book Award and the Foreword INDIES Book of the Year Bronze and Silver Awards. He teaches environmental studies, American literature, and creative writing at Pennsylvania State University's Altoona College.

Timothy Dodd is from Mink Shoals, West Virginia, and is the author of *Fissures, and Other Stories* (Bottom Dog Press). His stories have appeared in *Yemassee, Broad River Review, Glassworks Magazine,* and *Anthology of Appalachian Writers*; his poetry in *The Literary Review, Crab Creek Review, Roanoke Review,* and elsewhere. His second collection of stories, *Men in Midnight Bloom,* is forthcoming (Cowboy Jamboree Press), as are *Mortality Birds* (with Steve Lambert, Southernmost Books) and his first collection of poetry, *Modern Ancient* (High Window Press). Find him at timothybdodd.wordpress.com

Michael Dowdy is a poet, scholar, and essayist whose books include *Urbilly* (Main Street Rag Poetry Book Award), *Broken Souths* (University of Arizona Press), and, as coeditor with Claudia Rankine, *Poetics of Social Engagement* (Wesleyan University Press). Originally from Blacksburg, Virginia, he teaches at the University of South Carolina.

Hilda Downer is the author of three books of poetry and the forthcoming, Wiley's Last Resort, which includes poems about Wiley Quixote and SAWC gatherings. She is a long-term member of SAWC and the North Carolina Writers Conference. Her passion has been volunteer work in elementary schools to promote the reading and writing of poetry. She lives in Sugar Grove, North Carolina where she is retired, both as an English adjunct at Appalachian State University and as a psychiatric nurse.

Damian Dressick is the author of the novel *40 Patchtown* and the flash collection *Fables of the Deconstruction*. His writing has appeared in more than fifty literary journals and anthologies, including W.W. Norton's *New Micro*, *Electric Literature*, *Post Road*, *New Orleans Review*, *Cutbank*, *Smokelong Quarterly*, and *New World Writing*. A Blue Mountain Residency Fellow, Dressick is the winner of the Harriette Arnow Award and the Jesse Stuart Prize. He co-hosts WANA: LIVE! a (largely) virtual reading series that brings some of the best Appalachian writers to the world. Damian also serves as Editor-in-Chief for the journal *Appalachian Lit*. For more, check out www.damiandressick.com.

Sue Weaver Dunlap grew up East Tennessee and now lives deep in the Southern Appalachian Mountains near Walland, Tennessee, on a mountain farm. Here, she writes poetry, fiction, and memoir. Her poems have appeared in *Appalachian Journal* and *Southern Poetry Anthology*, among others. She has a chapbook *The Story Tender* (Finishing Line Press, 2014), a full collection entitled *Knead* (Main Street Rag, 2016), and another collection *A Walk to the Spring House* (Iris Press, 2021).

Gabriel Dunsmith's poems have also appeared in *Poetry*, *Kakalak*, and *On the Seawall*. He grew up in Asheville, North Carolina (in a family with deep roots in Grainger County, Tennessee), and attended Vassar College. He lives in Reykjavík, Iceland.

Dale Farmer produces films about Appalachian music and culture. His 2019 film, *The Mountain Minor*, was inspired by his grandparents' migration from Eastern Kentucky to Southwestern Ohio (themountainminormovie.com). Dale plays the banjo and fiddle in two bands and loves jamming around Cincinnati, at music festivals and on the front porch of his log cabin in the woods near Oxford, Ohio.

Nettie Farris is the author of four published chapbooks of poetry; most recently *The Alice Poems*, dancing girl press. Her interviews and reviews have appeared in *Heavy Feathers* and *North American Review*. Currently, she is experimenting with memoir and very short nonfiction.

Carol Grametbauer lives in Kingston, Tennessee, and is the author of two chapbooks: *Homeplace*, (Main Street Rag, 2018) and *Now & Then* (Finishing Line Press, 2014). Her poems have appeared in journals including *Appalachian Heritage*, *Appalachian Journal*, *Connecticut River Review*, *Pine Mountain Sand & Gravel*, *POEM*, and *The Sow's Ear Poetry Review*, and in a number of anthologies.

Connie Jordan Green lives on a farm in East Tennessee where she writes and gardens. She is the author of two award-winning novels for young people, two poetry chapbooks, and two poetry collections, most recently *Darwin's Breath* from Iris Press. She previously wrote a newspaper column that ran for over forty-two years. She frequently teaches writing workshops for various groups. Her poetry has been nominated for several Pushcart Awards.

Kari Gunter-Seymour is Ohio's Poet Laureate, the author of three books of poetry, a 2021 recipient of an Academy of American Poets Laureate Fellowship Award, the 2020 Ohio Poet of the year, editor of nine anthologies and an artist in residence for the Wexner Center for the Arts.

Richard Hague is a Northern Appalachian and life-long resident of urban and rural Ohio. He is an Editor Emeritus of *PMS&G* and editor of *Quarried: Three Decades of Pine Mt. Sand & Gravel* (Dos Madres Press 2015). His latest Book is *Earnest Occupations: Teaching, Writing, Gardening, & Other Local Work* (Bottom Dog Press, 2019).

A life-long resident of the Upper Ohio Valley, **William Scott Hanna** is an associate professor of English at West Liberty University in West Liberty, West Virginia, where he teaches creative writing, American Literature, and Appalachian Literature. His poetry and creative nonfiction has appeared in *Pine Mountain Sand and Gravel*, *Belt Magazine*, *Still: The Journal*, *Fourth & Sycamore*, and *I Thought I Heard a Cardinal Sing: Ohio's Appalachian Voices*.

Pauletta Hansel's newest poetry collection is *Heartbreak Tree*, an exploration of the intersection of gender and place in Appalachia. Her writing has been featured in *Oxford American*, *Rattle*, *American Life in Poetry*, and *Poetry Daily*, among others including *Palindrome*, which won the 2017 Weatherford Award for Poetry. Pauletta was Cincinnati's first Poet Laureate and is 2022 Writer-in-Residence for The Public Library of Cincinnati and Hamilton County.

Marc Harshman's *Woman in Red Anorak*, Blue Lynx Prize, was published in 2018 by Lynx House Press. His fourteenth children's book, *Fallingwater*, co-author, Anna Smucker, was published by Roaring Brook/Macmillan. His Thanksgiving poem, "Dispatch from the Mountain State," was printed in 2020 in *The New York Times*. Poems have been anthologized by Kent State University, University of Iowa, University of Georgia, and the University of Arizona.

Pamela Hirschler grew up in Eastern Kentucky, studied creative writing at Morehead State University, and received an MFA in Poetry from Drew University. Her poetry and reviews have previously appeared in *Pine Mountain Sand & Gravel, Still: The Journal, Tupelo Quarterly,* and other journals. Her first poetry chapbook collection, *What Lies Beneath*, was published in 2019 by Finishing Line Press.

Thomas Alan Holmes' research and creative work have appeared in such journals as *Louisiana Review, Valparaiso Poetry Review, The Connecticut Review, Appalachian Heritage, Blue Mesa Review, Still: The Journal,* and *Appalachian Journal*, as well as *Pine Mountain Sand and Gravel*. With Daniel Westover, he recently edited *The Fire That Breaks: Gerard Manley Hopkins's Poetic Legacies* (Clemson University Press, 2020). Alan and his family live in Johnson City, Tennessee, where he specializes in Appalachian and African American literature as a professor of English at East Tennessee State University. Iris Press will release his *In the Backhoe's Shadow*, a poetry collection, in summer 2022.

Byron Hoot has poems in *The Watershed Journal, Tobeco Literary Arts Journal*, and on www.northsouthappal.com./appalachian literature.html. Tiny Seed, Adelaide Press, *Keystone: An Anthology of Pennsylvania Poets* to be published by Penn State University Press. Co-founder of The Tamarack Writers (1974) and The Fernwood Writers Retreat (2019). Hootnhowlpoetry.com. Check out *Piercing the Veil, Appalachian Visions* among other volumes.

Patricia Hope's award-winning writing has appeared in *Chicken Soup for the Soul, Number One, Pigeon Parade Quarterly, 2021 Anthology of Appalachian Writers, The Mildred Haun Review, Liquid Imagination, American Diversity Report,* and many others. She lives in Oak Ridge, Tennessee.

Ron Houchin's latest book, *Talking to Shadows*, is his second book in the LSU Press's Southern Messenger Poets Series. He has eight other books of poetry published. His work has appeared in many journals and venues in Canada, Ireland, Wales as well as the US. His awards include the Weatherford Award and the Appalachian book of the year.

Scott T. Hutchison's previous work has appeared in *Pine Mountain Sand & Gravel, The Georgia Review* and *The Southern Review*. Poems are forthcoming in *Appalachian Heritage, Pine Mountain Sand & Gravel, Evening Street Review, Reckoning, Narrative Northeast,* and *Naugatuck River Review*. A new book of poetry, *Moonshine Narratives*, is available from Main Street Rag Publishing.

Judy Jenks is a nurse practitioner and college professor. She started photography and writing as a child but only recently has shared her work. She has been published in the Appalachian Journal and PMS&G. She wrote a monthly health column for the Native American magazine, *The Phoenix*. Judy holds a post-graduate certificate in Appalachian Studies from Radford University.

LuLu Johnson earned an MFA in Poetry from Georgia State University where she had the pleasure of learning from David Bottoms. She began writing personal lyrical essays without knowing what they were until David Shields told her at Bread Loaf Writers Conference. This essay is from a series she's begun called "Horses I Have Known."

Jackie Ison Kalbli writes poems where she can see horses out the window, let the weeds grow, and ponder the wonder of living long enough to consider herself an elder.

Natalie Kimbell lives in Sequatchie County, Tennessee. She is a mother of two, and a grandmother of four. She works as a teacher of English, creative theater, and creative writing at her high school alma mater. Her poetry is published in *The 2019 Chattanooga Writers' Guild Anthology*, and *The 2020 Garfield Lake Review*, *The 2020 Chattanooga Writers' Guild Anthology*, the 2021 *Appalachian Writers Anthology, Dorothy Allison Version* and *The American Diversity Report*. Her work also appears in the 2021/22 Women of Appalachia Project's *Women Speak* anthology, *Beautiful: In the Eye of the Beholder,* and *Abyss and Apex,* April 2022.

Patsy Kisner's poems have appeared in journals such as *Appalachian Journal, Forge, Spoon River Poetry Review* and *The Red Moon Anthology*. She is the author of a poetry chapbook, *Inside the Horse's Eye*, and a poetry collection, *Last Days of an Old Dog*, both from Finishing Line Press.

Carol Parris Krauss enjoys using place/nature as theme vehicles. Her poetry can be found at *Louisiana Literature, Scrawl Place, The Skinny Poetry Journal, The South Carolina*

Review, Story South, and *Broadkill Review.* She was honored to be recognized as a Best New Poet by the *University of Virginia Press*. In 2021, she won the Eastern Shore Writers Association *Crossroads Contest* and her chapbook, *Just a Spit Down the Road* was published by Kelsay Books.

Dan Leach has published poetry and short fiction in *The New Orleans Review*, *Smokelong Quarterly*, and *The Sun*. His short story "Wasp Queen" was recently awarded the Editors' Prize at Copper Nickel. He holds an MFA from Warren Wilson.

John C. Mannone, a retired physicist in Knoxville, TN, has poems in *North Dakota Quarterly*, *Le Menteur*, *Poetry South*, and others. A Jean Ritchie Fellowship winner in Appalachian literature (2017), he served as celebrity judge for the NFSPS (2018). His poetry won the Impressions of Appalachia Creative Arts Contest (2020). He edits poetry for *Abyss & Apex* and other journals. http://jcmannone.wordpress.com | https://www.facebook.com/jcmannone

Preston Martin has published poems in *New Ohio Review, Iodine, Tar River Poetry, Chaffin Journal, Kakalak, Broad River Review, Appalachian Review, Pine Mountain Sand & Gravel* and other journals. He has poems in *Every River on Earth: Writings from Appalachian Ohio* (Ohio University Press) and other anthologies. He lives in Chapel Hill, North Carolina.

Alexandra McIntosh lives and writes in Kentucky, her favorite place in the world. Her debut book of poetry, *Bowlfuls of Blue,* is available from Assure Press. She received her BA from Asbury University, her MA in English from Northern Kentucky University, and her MFA in Poetry from Miami University.

Alexandra currently serves as Managing Editor of *Moon Cola Zine*. You can find links to her publications and pictures of her dog on her website AlexandraMcIntosh.com.

Llewellyn McKernan has an MA in writing from Brown University. She has authored six poetry books for adults and four for children, with poems published in many journals and fifty anthologies. Her work has won eighty awards in state, regional, and national contests. Appalachia's her home because writing poems is "always home" to her and she's written more poetry there than anywhere on earth.

Denise Roberts McKinney grew up playing in the sacred woods of the Daniel Boone National Forest in Jackson County, Kentucky. Currently living in Berea, Kentucky, she is a woman of few words, but one who still plays in the woods and enjoys laughter as a daily tonic.

Wendy McVicker is the 2020-2023 poet laureate of Athens OH, and a longtime teaching artist. Her most recent chapbook is *Zero, a Door* (The Orchard Street Press, 2021). She has appeared before in *Pine Mountain Sand & Gravel*. She loves collaborating with other artists, and has been known to perform with musician Emily Prince, under the name *another language altogether*.

Clarksburg, West Virginia native **Donna Meredith** is Associate Editor of *Southern Literary Review*. Her award-winning novels include *Buried Seeds, The Glass Madonna, The Color of Lies, Wet Work and Fraccidental Death,* and she wrote one nonfiction title, *Magic in the Mountains*. Donna graduated from Fairmont State College, West Virginia University, and Nova Southeastern and studied creative writing at Florida State.

Karla Linn Merrifield has had 1000+ poems appear in dozens of journals and anthologies. She has 15 books to her credit. Following her 2018 *Psyche's Scroll* (Poetry Box Select) is the full-length book *Athabaskan Fractal: Poems of the Far North* from Cirque Press. Her newest poetry collection, *My Body the Guitar*, inspired by famous guitarists and their guitars was published in December 2021 by Before Your Quiet Eyes Publications Holograph Series (Rochester, NY). She is a frequent contributor to *The Songs of Eretz Poetry Review*.
Website: https://www.karlalinnmerrifield.org/; blog at https://karlalinnmerrifield.wordpress.com/; Tweet @LinnMerrifiel; Instagram: https://www.facebook.com/karlalinn.merrifield.

Jennifer Davis Michael is a professor of English at the University of the South in Sewanee, Tennessee, at the tip of the Cumberland Plateau. She is the author of two chapbooks from Finishing Line Press: *Let Me Let Go* (2020) and *Dubious Breath* (2022). Her website is jenniferdavismichael.com.

Jim Minick is the author of five books, the most recent, *Fire Is Your Water,* a novel. *The Blueberry Years*, his memoir, won the Best Nonfiction Book of the Year from Southern Independent Booksellers Association. His work has appeared in many publications including *The New York Times, Poets & Writers, Tampa Review, Shenandoah, Orion, Oxford American,* and *The Sun*. His latest, *Spin: Three Tornados and a Pair of Ruby Slippers*, is forthcoming from the University of Nebraska Press.

Karen Whittington Nelson writes poetry and fiction from her home on a small Southeastern Ohio farm. Her work has been published in the anthology, *I Thought I Heard a Cardinal Sing: Ohio's Appalachian Voices*, *Sheila-Na-Gig Online*, *Northern Appalachia Review*, Women of Appalachia Project's *Women*

Speak Volumes 2–7, *Anthology of Appalachian Writers, Gyroscope Review* and *Pudding Magazine.*

Elaine Fowler Palencia, originally from Morehead, Kentucky, has authored six books of fiction, four poetry chapbooks, and a nonfiction book, *On Rising Ground: The Life and Civil War Letters of John M. Douthit, 52nd Georgia Volunteer Infantry* (Mercer U. Press, 2021). She is the book review editor of *Pegasus*, journal of the Kentucky State Poetry Society.

Chrissie Anderson Peters is a native of Tazewell, Virginia. She lives in Bristol, Tennessee, with her husband and their four feline children. A graduate of Emory & Henry College and the University of Tennessee, she has written three books (*Dog Days and Dragonflies, Running From Crazy,* and *Blue Ridge Christmas*), and has a forthcoming collection due out later in 2022. Her passions include music (especially 80s) and travel. Her website is www.CAPWrites.com.

Jay Pettit worked in insurance and construction. For several years he was a participant in the Community of Creative Writers Ohio River Retreat sponsored by Thomas More University. Jay was a devoted son, brother, husband, father, student, and seeker of all things spiritual.

Rhonda Pettit, PhD, is a professor of English at the University of Cincinnati Blue Ash College, and editor of the *Blue Ash Review*. Her most recent book of poems is *Riding the Wave Train* (Dos Madres Press, 2017). She is currently at work on several creative projects.

Gary Phillips is the 2016-2018 poet laureate of Carrboro, North Carolina. He lives in a rammed earth house he built with friends.

A child of Appalachia, Gary reads poetry and Afro-Futurism, studies amphibian activities on full moon nights. His book of poetry and occasional pieces, *The Boy The Brave Girls* was printed in 2016 by Human Error Publishing (Wendell, Mass).

Karl Plank is a North Carolina poet. His work has appeared in publications such as *Still, Zone 3, New Madrid, Beloit Poetry Journal, Notre Dame Review*, and has been featured on *Poetry Daily*. He is the Cannon Professor of Religion at Davidson College.

Sherry Poff enjoyed an idyllic childhood in the hills of West Virginia. She now lives and writes in and around Chattanooga, Tennessee, and is an active member of the Chattanooga Writers' Guild. Her stories and poems have appeared recently in *Raconteur Review, Bluepepper, Heart of Flesh, Speckled Trout Review*, and *The Chattanooga Pulse*.

Matt Prater is a writer from Saltville, Virginia. His work has appeared in *Spillway, Poet Lore, Hampden-Sydney Poetry Review*, and *Still: The Journal*, among this and other publications. He has recently completed a PhD in Comparative Studies from Florida Atlantic University, where his dissertation work was focused on Appalachian literature in an international context.

Dale Marie Prenatt is from southern West Virginia by way of east Kentucky. She earned a bachelor's degree in Theatre from Morehead State. Her poems have appeared in journals and the anthologies *I Thought I Heard a Cardinal Sing, Appalachian Reckoning,* and *Quarried*. She is learning the ukulele and manages a bookstore in Cincinnati.

Phyllis Price is a Virginia-based writer rooted in Appalachia. Her work has appeared in numerous journals and anthologies, including *Anthology of Appalachian Writers, Volume XII, Appalachian Heritage, Connecticut River Review, The Bluestone Review, Poem,* and others. Publication credits include the chapbook *Quarry Song* and spiritual autobiography *Holy Fire.* Price lives on a small farm with two sheep, five goats, and seven laying hens.

Bonnie Proudfoot hails from New York, moved to West Virginia in 1979, and has made her home in Athens, Ohio, since 1996. Her poetry and short fiction has appeared in various journals, including *Pine Mountain Sand and Gravel, Rattle,* and *Kestrel.* Her first novel, *Goshen Road,* (Swallow Press, 2020), was long-listed for the PEN/ Hemingway award and received the WCONA Book of the Year award. Her first chapbook of poems, *Household Gods* (Sheila-Na-Gig) is forthcoming in the summer of 2022. When the spirit moves her, Bonnie works on glass art in her Athens studio.

A. Riel Regan has been a passionate and observant reader and writer for as long as they can remember. They're a recent graduate of Thomas More University from Oldham County, Kentucky, and are excitedly turning their eyes toward the publishing world. They're currently workshopping their entire body of work up to this point and beginning on several chapbooks. They offer editing and cover design services for writers at https://reddest.wixsite.com/redinkscrawl.

McKenna Revel is a writer from Eastern Kentucky. For someone who doesn't consider herself a poet, she writes an awful lot of poetry. She resides with her fiancé, her dogs, and her cat. All are looking forward to another intimate living room reading, according to her.

Taylor Roberts lives in her native southwest Virginia with her husband and daughter in their beloved single wide trailer. Her most practical education has been a life spent outdoors in the company of her grandparents and great grandparents. She hopes her writing does justice to their struggles and triumphs.

Tommye Scanlin is Professor Emerita at the University of North Georgia, Dahlonega. She is a member of Southern Highland Craft Guild and has exhibited her tapestries widely. Scanlin is the author of *The Nature of Things: Essays of a Tapestry Weaver* and *Tapestry Design Basics and Beyond: Planning and Weaving with Confidence.*

Mike Schoeffel is a writer and firefighter based in Western North Carolina. His work has appeared in *USA Today*, *Little Patuxent Review*, *Bookends Review*, *Sheepshead Review*, *Non-Conformist Mag*, *Firefighter Nation* and a short story collection published by Propertius Press titled "Draw Down the Moon." In addition to his published short stories and essays, he's also working on a novel titled "All the Hungry Islands," a semi-autobiographical meditation on the birth of his son, Conley, who has a rare genetic disorder called Van Maldergem Syndrome. He runs the online magazine, *Ourland* (ourlandmag.com). His online portfolio can be found at mikeschoeffelwriter.wordpress.com.

Roberta Schultz, author of four chapbooks, is a songwriter and poet from Wilder, Kentucky. She writes some of her songs on a mountain in North Carolina. She is co-founder of the Poet & Song House Concert Series with her Raison D'Etre trio mates. You can find out way more than you'd ever want to know about her at these websites: robertaschultz.com and raison3.com.

Ann Shurgin is a native of Elizabethton, Tennessee, and has been a SAWC member since 2001. She lived in southeast Texas for many years, working as a writer and editor. She returned home to the mountains after retirement and now lives in the house she grew up in. Her first book of poetry, *While the Whippoorwill Called*, was published in 2022.

Sherrie A. Skipper writes between her studio in Oxford, Ohio, and LA. She has an MA in spiritual psychology and has enjoyed being a scribe with camera, notebook and crayons since childhood. Her chapbook, *Somewhere Between Witchcraft and Miracles*, and other writings can be found at sherrieskipper.com.

Gerald Smith is the author/editor of several volumes of university history and Appalachian place studies. Smith has spent more than a quarter century studying rural life including farms, churches, log structures and cemeteries. His poetry concerns the sense of loss and displacement in Appalachian settings.

Anna Egan Smucker's *No Star Nights* (Knopf) won the International Reading Association Children's Book Award. *Fallingwater* was co-authored with Marc Harshman, and two of her nine books represented West Virginia at the National Book Festival. With poems in anthologies and literary journals, her chapbook, *Rowing Home*, was published by Finishing Line Press. She calls Bridgeport, West Virginia home.

Philip St. Clair's ninth collection of poetry, *Red Cup, Green Lawn*, was published by Main Street Rag in 2020. He has received fellowships from the NEA and the Kentucky Arts Council and was awarded the Bullis Prize from *Poetry Northwest*. He has loaded aircraft in the United States Air Force, mopped floors in a student union, tended bar in an Elks club, worked at the editor's trade, and taught at three universities and a community college.

Sherry Cook Stanforth is the founder/director of Originary Arts Initiative, providing regional arts- and nature-inspired programming for diverse populations. She is the managing editor of *Pine Mountain Sand & Gravel* and *Riparian: Poems, Short Prose, and Photographs Inspired by the Ohio River* (Dos Madres Press, 2019). Her poetry collection *Drone String* (Bottom Dog Press, 2015) reflects the storytelling and music traditions of her Appalachian heritage. She performs in two bands, Tellico and Tangled Roots, and enjoys hiking, beekeeping and studying native plants. Originaryartsinitiative@gmail.com

Eugene Stevenson, son of immigrants, father of expatriates, lives in the mountains of western North Carolina. His chapbook, The Population of Dreams (Finishing Line Press), debuted 2022. His poems have appeared in *After Hours Journal*, *Angel City Review*, *The Hudson Review*, *San Pedro River Review*, *Tipton Poetry Journal*, *Washington Square Review* & others.

A. E. Stringer is the author of four collections of poems, including *Asbestos Brocade* (Salmon Poetry, 2017). His work has appeared in such journals as *The Nation, Antaeus, The Ohio Review, Denver Quarterly,* and *Prairie Schooner.* He also edited and introduced an edition of Louise McNeill's *Paradox Hill* (West Virginia University Press, 2009). For twenty-four years, he taught writing and literature at Marshall University in Huntington, West Virginia.

Chuck Stringer is grateful to have spent another year writing with fellow regional poets in the Thomas More University Creative Writing Vision Program. His work has been published in *For a Better World*, *Literary Accents*, *Pine Mountain Sand & Gravel*, *Riparian*, *The Licking River Review*, and *Words*. He lives with wife Susan in a house near Fowlers Fork in Union, Kentucky.

Thomas E. Strunk grew up in Minisink Hills, Pennsylvania, on the Delaware River. His work explores nature and working-class life and strives to express the longing for spiritual, emotional, and political liberation. His literary work has appeared or is forthcoming in *Pinyon*, *Dash*, *Anthology of Appalachian Writers*, *Northern Appalachia Review* and *East Fork Journal*. Thomas blogs at LiberationNow.org.

Michael Templeton is an independent scholar, writer, and musician. He completed his PhD in literary studies at Miami University in 2005. He has published scholarly studies, cultural analysis, and creative non-fiction. He currently works as a freelance writer providing articles for the Urban Appalachian Community Coalition in Cincinnati. He lives in Cincinnati, Ohio with his wife, who is an artist.

Michael Thompson is a multimedia artist, ethnographer, and poet. He takes on the role of artist as archivist; collecting things, spaces, and histories to add to his work and life. His practice focuses on human ecology and nuance as well as the philosophy of nature, space, and built reality. His current work has found him using painting, ethnography, architecture, and poetry in his multi-year project, *"Sanctuaries."*

Ann Thornfield-Long is a retired nurse and first responder, former editor-publisher of *The Norris Bulletin*, a weekly newspaper and is co-author of *Tennessee Women of Vision and Courage*, (Smiley and Crawford, 2013.) She has poetry in *Artemis Journal*, *Riddled with Arrows*, *Liquid Imagination*, *Pigeon Parade* and others, and has nominations for Best of the Net, Pushcart and Rhysling Awards.

Allison Thorpe's latest collection is *Reckless Pilgrims* (Broadstone Books). She works as a writing mentor for the Carnegie Center and lives in Lexington, Kentucky.

Dorothy Weil is a long-time writer, publishing fiction, scholarly work, a memoir, and features in newspapers and magazines throughout the country. She served as writer-producer with TV IMAGE, creating a dozen documentaries. She is now concentrating on poetry. With the help of a friend, Weil is trying to locate a permanent home for the collar (featured in this issue of *PMS&G*) that she has kept safe for so many years.

Dick Westheimer has—with his wife and writing companion Debbie—lived on their plot of land in rural southwest Ohio for over 40 years. His most recent poems have appeared or are upcoming in *Rattle*, *Minyan*, *Gyroscope Review*, *Cutthroat*, *Paterson Review*, and the anthology *I Thought I Heard a Cardinal Sing*.

Laurie Wilcox-Meyer's chapbook, *Circling Silence,* was published in 2018 by Finishing Line Press. Her full-length book of poetry, *Of Wilderness and Flight*, was published in 2019 by FootHills Publishing. *Conversation in the Key Of Blue,* her latest collection, was published by Main Street Rag Publishing, 2020. Laurie Wilcox-Meyer lives in the French Broad River basin in the Blue Ridge Mountains of North Carolina where she often spots bears while hiking and meditating about her next poem.

Dana Wildsmith's newest collection of poetry, *With Access to Tools*, is forthcoming from Madville Publishing in 2023. Wildsmith is the author of five additional collections of poetry, a novel, and an environmental memoir. She has served as Artist-in-Residence for Grand Canyon National Park and Everglades National Park, and she is a Fellow of the Hambidge Center for Creative Arts and Sciences.

Elissa Yancey, MSEd, is seasoned writer, educator and nonprofit leader. An Urban Appalachian, she was born and raised in Norwood, Ohio—a city surrounded by Cincinnati that has remained fiercely independent, like many of its mountain-born residents. Her memoir-in-essays, *Grab Happy*, details her 12-year caregiving journey with her mom, Gladys Yancey, who died in 2010.

John Thomas York's poetry collection, *Cold Spring Rising*, was published in 2012 by Press 53. His work has recently appeared in *Tar River Poetry*, *Cold Mountain Review*, *Appalachian Journal*, and *Pine Mountain Sand & Gravel*. He has won both the James Applewhite Poetry Prize and the Alex Albright Creative Nonfiction Prize from *North Carolina Literary Review*.

Submission Guidelines

Volume 26:
The Strange, Stranger, & Estranged Side of Appalachia

Deadline: April 15, 2023
Response: Late June, 2023
Publication Date: October 2023

Such a strange, strange world—what person, place, or thing exists to catch your eye or transfix your mind? What experience, in all of its unusual glory, startles you? Exhilarates you? And, as we imagine with regional spirit, even *stranger* things may emerge on the horizon to shape our day, or even the rest of our lives. Strange (if not delightfully odd) to some of us—funnel clouds, pawpaws, foxfire, sinkholes, hellbenders, weather, pandemics, watermelon pickles, blood rain, mimosa trees, cuckoos, the bowed psaltery, moonbows, old spinning wheels. Perhaps even stranger—James Still's brief portrait of Walking John Gay in *River of Earth*, the transformative power of shape note singing, water hemlock springing across Ohio's fields. Bridge ghosts. Sediment ponds. That time when "the moon shall turn to blood." Collectanea stored by giant packrats. A mold-slickened earthen basement in a North Georgia home along the Star Route. Ginseng magic. Sorrow seeds planted along the Trail of Tears, upon slave auction blocks, inside the US Capitol on January 6th, 2021.

The boundary line dividing the familiar from the unfamiliar is elusive. And, as they say, *strange* doesn't always mean *bad*. The centuries-old Latin term *extraneus* recalls what exists on the outside—unpredictable people, places, and circumstances. Some things are just too weird or wonderful to be a coincidence. What, or who, we encounter on our paths invites our energetic interpretation. Will you welcome the stranger who may come to call? Or refuse to embrace her/him/they? That stranger in our midst—misfit, or outsider, or an estranged loved one we "used to know" or "thought we knew"—exists to challenge our sense of being in the world.

Strangeness follows us wherever we go. And so our poems, short stories, testimonies, and art images for Volume 26 begin to unfurl…

We mostly accept unpublished work, but we aren't sticklers. We feature solicited reviews of recent books by Appalachian writers, especially those who have already published work in *PMS&G*. We are happy to consider unsolicited reviews, too. Finally, if your book or chapbook is published within our issue year, we invite you to share a brief description with us for our New Books section. Full guidelines for submitting to *PMS&G* can be found here: http://www.sawconline.net/pmsg-submission-guidelines.html or emailed upon request to pmsg.journal@gmail.com.

PLEASE, PLEASE, PLEASE follow our specific guidelines if you would like for us to consider your submission. Work pasted directly into the email message or sent as PDF attachment, or in other fonts or formatting is very time-consuming for our editing and layout process. This makes us cranky. So does opening up a bunch of documents from the same person, or tracing unlabeled pieces back to their author's email. And you don't want cranky editors, now, do you?